A THREAD OF SCARLET

This is the story of Donald Campbell, a young Scottish priest, from his ordination to his death as a Cardinal. In his rise through the hierarchy he travels widely and observes shrewdly " the world's slow stain " in the actions of many people, laymen and churchmen alike, in many lands, but he himself remains unspotted by the world. Only the good, as a famous religious writer has remarked, can properly understand evil, and Donald Campbell is a good man for whom the glory of God and the truth and beauty of his Faith abide despite everything as the ultimate realities.

A Thread of Scarlet is an appropriate successor to *Father Malachy's Miracle*, *All Glorious Within*, *Yellow Tapers for Paris*, etc., which have established the author in the minds of hundreds of thousands of readers as one of the foremost contemporary Catholic novelists.

Bruce Marshall

A THREAD OF
SCARLET

COLLINS
ST. JAMES'S PLACE, LONDON
1959

FOR LESLIE

who may one day read this book

" Thy lips are like a thread of scarlet, and thy speech is comely."

THE SONG OF SOLOMON

" Quand nous ne parlons pas à Dieu ou pour Dieu, c'est au diable que nous parlons, et il nous écoute dans un formidable silence."

LÉON BLOY: *Pélérin de l' Absolu*

Author's Foreword

With the exception of the two Popes, to whom invented conversations have been attributed, all the characters in this novel are imaginary. The names of my two Archbishops of Inchkeith and the Pentlands have been used solely because of the feud between the clans, and no reference is intended to apply to any Scottish Archbishop, living or dead.

For permission to quote from the English translation of Kierkegaard's works I am grateful to the translator, Mr. W. H. Auden, and the publishers, Messrs. Cassells.

B. M.

CHAPTER I

THE ARCHBISHOP was leaving for Paris the same morning and had to make his new priests quickly. He was waiting vested in the sanctuary when the deacons processed in in their albs and white stoles. It was the feast of St. Cyril of Jerusalem 1907, the day Maud Allan danced Salome before King Edward.

Donald Dunwhinnie Campbell's name was conspicuous among the others called out by Canon Poustie: Ryans and Byrnes whom birth in the Archdiocese of Inchkeith and the Pentlands had enabled to pass as Scotsmen in the Church of God.

" *Quoniam, fratres carissimi, rectori navis . . .*" The fragrance of their lives must be a delight to Christ's Assembly, the Archbishop told the deacons. Then he laid his hands on their heads and Canon Poustie and Fathers O'Callaghan, Weir and Scully laid their hands on the young men's heads too. The Archbishop prayed that the spirit might be poured into them as into Eleazar and Ithamar. Then he crossed their stoles on their breasts, anointed their hands with the oil of catechumens and bound them, and the deacons were priests.

Through the Church, the Archbishop reminded

them in his allocution, God had taught men as much about Himself as He dared. Baptism, penance, eucharist, at these they could never fail. For the rest, what they did would always be more important than what they said: a Church which had survived the crowning of Napoleon by Pius VII would get over a mistake or two about the Trinity in a sermon. They must be able to distinguish between sentiment and sentimentality. They must not allow their celibacy to chill their love for their fellow men. If they got themselves hated they must see that they didn't get God hated too: St. Francis of Sales had been canonised because of the patience with which he had listened to bores. They must read secular books as well as religious, so as to know what the enemies of the Church were saying and thinking.

They must not be discouraged by the imperfections which they would certainly encounter in their colleagues and in their superiors: it was only in the Church Triumphant that all bishops were holy and intelligent and all priests humble and wise. In the meantime they must put up with being cogs in the century-slow machinery of grace, unknown members of the Church Militant from Laurence on his grid to Mrs. O'Flaherty offering up her ingrowing toenail.

Finally, the Archbishop said, they were to remember that probably not more than ten per cent of Christians were saved, and that clergymen were not inevitably of their number. For that reason they must be able

to answer rightly on their death beds the question
from the liturgy of St. John Chrysostom: " Have I
taken care to seek a blameless life and a good defence
before the dread judgment seat of Christ?"

2

" Why are you not out blessing your family and
your friends with the others?" the Archbishop asked
Father Campbell when he saw him self-consciously
studying the notice

NOMEN ARCIEPISCOPI:

JOANNIS

hung above the vestment chest in the sacristy to
remind visiting priests to pray for the Most Reverend
John Angus MacDonald after Puis X in the *Te igitur*.
" I've nobody, Your Grace. I'm a convert, you
see, and my parents don't exactly approve," the
young priest said, blushing at having to talk about
his hurt.
" In that case you'd better try your hand on me,
Father." The Archbishop was down on his knees
before Father Campbell could stop him. " I remember
now. You're the one that's come back from Rome.
Well, why did you join us? Because you wanted to
believe as much as possible? Or to see how little you
need believe without falling into heresy?"

" Newman, isn't that, Your Grace? "

" Good for you. A believer's a man who distrusts his doubts more than his beliefs and an unbeliever's a man who distrusts his beliefs more than his doubts. And what did you say your name was again? "

" Campbell, Your Grace. Donald Campbell."

" Let's hope the 'Donald' will save you. The Campbells murdered thirty-six MacDonalds at Glencoe in 'ninety-two and I had only three pipers at my consecration because the fourth was a Campbell and refused to turn out."

Canon Poustie came fussing up.

" Your train, Your Grace," he said.

"Just a moment, Canon. I'm talking to the laddie. Where are you staying, Father? Not with your parents it seems? "

" No, Your Grace. At the Thistle Hotel."

" Nice and handy, although I don't know that St. Paul would have sent Timothy there. And what's your French like? "

" Fair, Your Grace."

" Not as good as your Italian, eh? But I expect it's good enough for me. I'm off to Paris this morning for the funeral of an Auxiliary there and I could do with an interpreter. How would you like to come with me? We can collect your luggage on the way. All right. Off with those priestly vestments now. We haven't all that time to lose."

Too excited to thank the Archbishop properly, Father Campbell scrambled out of his vestments and followed the Archbishop and Canon Poustie along the underground passage connecting the pro-cathedral with the clergy house.

The Archdiocese of Inchkeith and the Pentlands was too poor to afford a private residence for its Ordinary, and the second-floor of the clergy-house had to do for his palace. The Archbishop's study was hung with portraits of his predecessors and of misty Vicars Apostolic all looking like Prince Charlie. A red-haired young priest with a beefy face was waiting there.

" I've rung up the Franciscans, Your Grace, and the Prior is quite willing for Father Gregory to be given second helpings while he's in charge of the mission at Inverbervie," he said. " And here's the twenty pounds from the Union Bank, Your Grace. Balance after withdrawal one hundred and eleven pounds seventeen shillings and sixpence."

" That'll not buy me my new sanctuary." Helped by Canon Poustie, the Archbishop was getting out of his lace and purple silk. " Anything more about Major McGlashan ? "

" Yes, Your Grace. It turns out he's a Christian Scientist and now he says he doesn't know whether his dog's paw's been cured by his prayers or our ointment."

" Our ointment, of course."

13

" And, Your Grace, about the rosary at St. Cuthburga's . . ."

" Rosary indeed! The rosary's ruining us. Tell Father Scanlan that with my compliments. And now my bag, Father, if you don't mind. No, I don't want anybody to come to the station. You and the Canon'll be seeing more than enough of me again in less than a week."

3

The Archbishop waited outside the Thistle Hotel while Father Campbell paid his bill, and then they walked to the tram stop carrying their bags.

" Laddie, laddie, did nobody ever tell you you were hentoed? " the Archbishop said. " Forgive me for being personal, Father, but when you know me better you'll realise I'm always at it. When poor old Jimmie Stuart died there were two Scottish dioceses vacant and the clergy of both made a novena they wouldn't get me. Needless to say Inchkeith and the Pentlands lost."

Father Campbell smiled gently: less than half-an-hour ago God had put part of Himself into his hands for the rest of his life, and he wanted to think rather than to talk.

" Baron Von Hügel speaks of institutional Christianity as his hair shirt. If you don't know why, Father, you'll soon find out. But it's as necessary for religion as a bottle is for wine. The mistake people make is thinking they're expected to drink the bottle too. What they don't understand is that you've got to have the Form to hold the Spirit and the Spirit to fill the Form. Neither's much good without the other. Scotland's got the Spirit all right—you've only got to look at the decent faces you see in the street to see that; but the only place it's got the Form is in pokey wee pro-cathedrals like ours stuck in between billiard saloons and fish-and-chip shops. Spain and France and Italy have all got the Form but as far as I can see there's precious little Spirit about. In other words the world's going to rack and ruin because Protestants love their neighbour without loving God and Catholics love God without loving their neighbour." The shaggy face was turned, haggard with beseeching loneliness. "You do understand, Father, don't you?"

"Of course, Your Grace. The two great commandments."

"And they've *both* got to be kept, Father. I'll never apologise for our religion; but I often feel like apologising for us. It's no use our patting ourselves on the back for the religion *about* Jesus and then neglecting the religion *of* Jesus. Wiseman was more right than he thought when he warned his priests that they would find the Anglican clergy their superiors in everything except the possession of the Deposit of Faith. It's not only Latin and Greek the schismatics are better at; it's plain down-to-earth Pauline charity."

A car came up to the tram stop as they reached it, and the conductor helped them aboard with their bags. The rocky-faced passengers under the stained glass advertisments for Bovril and Wincarnis glowered at the Archbishop and Father Campbell as they sat down.

" The day they don't scowl, that is the day I'll be afraid," the Archbishop said and took out his breviary, leaving Father Campbell free to get on with his thinking.

4

" Having the right sort of religion is no excuse for writing the wrong sort of English," the Archbishop growled as he handed the *Catholic Trumpet* across the compartment to Father Campbell. " I shouldn't be surprised if this paper has made more people lose their faith than Robert Blatchford. *Catholic Strumpet* it ought to be called."

The man reading *London Life* winked at the man reading *The Garden of Allah* and held out his paper to the Archbishop.

" Perhaps your Reverence would like a wee read at this," he said.

The Archbishop smiled and shook his head.

" Thank you. On the whole, I think not," he said.

" Frightened to look at the lassies, are you?" The lean Lowland mouth shot out across the compartment like a confectioner's scoop. " Well, let me tell you you're wrong. ' For when they rise from the dead, they neither marry, nor are given in marriage,' it says in the Bible, doesn't it? And what'll you do then, old cock, I'd like to know."

" Try to get there before you, young cock, I expect," the Archbishop said.

" He's got you there, Geordie," the man with *The Garden of Allah* said.

" He hasn't got me at all," the man with *London Life* said. " I'm simply not interested in religion, that's all. And what's more neither was my poor dead father either."

" Don't worry," the Archbishop said. " He will be now."

" Funny, aren't we?" The man laid down *London Life* and took up the *Daily Standard*. " *Why Has the Church Failed?* it says here. Well if you don't know, I'll tell you. It's because of science. It's because the Pope doesn't know which came first: the egg or the chicken."

" There's no need to be rude to the gentleman, Geordie," a wrung-out woman next him said.

" I must say that I agree with our friend," a pale eager young man said. " In *The Golden Bough* Frazer makes it perfectly clear that all religions have their

17   B

origin in fear and the desire to propitiate unseen powers presumed to be unkind and malicious."

"Why can't the false be partial proof of the true rather than a total proof that the true itself is false?" the Archbishop asked. "Why has a fish never preached to other fish or a pig to other pigs? And why aren't those monkeys still evolving?"

"You're wrang," the man with *London Life* said. "And even if you prove you're richt you'll still be wrang."

The woman next him laughed loudest of them all.

By the time they passed the cold unsacramented Cathedral of York they were all friends, and the Archbishop was telling them that the Battle of Killiecrankie had not, as people imagined, been fought at the Soldier's Leap, but in the field behind.

5

The Archbishop himself served Father Campbell's first Mass in Westminster Cathedral next morning.

"You'll do fine," the old man told him when he had finished. "For my own part I'm like poor George Tyrrell: I find it more devotional to hear Mass than to say it. I've always forgiven that man because of his understanding Oscar Wilde. He said he'd rather have written *De Profundis* than the Epistle to the Thessalonians."

But it was of Robert Hugh Benson that the Cardinal

started to talk when they sat down to breakfast with him and his chaplain.

"If Hugh goes on the way he's doing, what with those books and sermons of his, we'll have the High Church party coming over in a body," the Cardinal said across the grilled tomatoes which so nearly matched his sash.

"People have been saying that since Newman came in, Your Eminence," the Archbishop said.

"I know, Your Grace. But things have changed since then. Nobody takes Protestantism seriously any longer—least of all Protestants."

"I just can't believe that, Your Eminence. Otherwise why are the inhabitants of Stockholm so much more honest than those of Naples?"

"That's no answer, Your Grace. Just imagine what Neapolitans would have been like if they had been Wesleyan Methodists."

"I think that we are all of us going to be grateful to Wesley one of these days," the Archbishop said. "And to the Church of England and the Church of Scotland too. If things go on the way they're doing soon it'll be agnosticism and not the sects that are the challenge."

"Quite," said the Cardinal. "And to meet that challenge Christianity will have to be taught as a metaphysical absolute. To do that you must have unquestionable authority. Which the Church of England lacks even more ostentatiously than the other sects. That's why we're making all those converts."

" Only among those who are Christians already," the Archbishop said. " Only among people who realise that the conduct of a minority of saints down the ages has proved that the Church is doing something more than trading on the possibility of some sort of marginal error between science and superstition. What about those who take us for charlatans and are genuinely unable to believe? It's them we've got to be able to answer. And it's no good telling them that faith is superior to reason or any of that sort of blether. We've got to be able to give our reasons for not reasoning."

" You'll be saying next that Almighty God ought to have summoned us one by one before our birth and told each one of us personally exactly what the consequences of our misconduct on earth would be," the Cardinal said.

" Mebbe it wouldn't have been such a bad idea, Your Eminence."

Father Campbell tried not to notice the slow wink the chaplain gave him over the egg he was digging at with his spoon.

" It would have meant that our faith would have been without merit, Your Grace," the Cardinal said. " Our virtue would have been merely a precaution, like taking out an insurance policy or saving up for old age."

"That's still no answer to Davey Hume," the Archbishop said.

"How many times have I got to tell you, Father, that the only way to take the top off an egg is with a knife," the Cardinal snapped as a spurt of yolk from the chaplain's egg shot on to the tablecloth.

"Hume said that all the knowledge we could ever have of ourselves boiled down to perception," the Archbishop said. "Perception of heat, cold, light, shade, pain, or pleasure. In other words the most that we can ever perceive is perception."

"We can go further, Your Grace, I think. We can perceive that we perceive the perception."

"Still with our material brain, Your Eminence. All that our material brain can remember is the memory of perceptions. And as that material brain dissolves when we die, Hume and his followers find it difficult to believe in the survival of the perceiver after death."

"The man was a heretic, that's all," the Cardinal said.

"A *Scots* heretic, Your Eminence. And one that the Hierarchy of England and Wales will have to answer if they're going to convert the readers of Shaw and Wells. And it'll be no use telling them that in A.D.543 St. Benedict saw St. Scholastica's soul flying to heaven in the shape of a dove either."

"And John Knox, Your Grace?" the Cardinal asked. "Will the Hierarchy of England and Wales have to answer him too?"

"John Knox wasn't as bad as he was painted, Your Eminence. He was right in hating the abuses he condemned. His mistake was in trying to *invent* a theology based on the nominalistic teaching of heretics. I'm not quite sure that I know what that means, but it must be right, because I read it in the *Tablet*."

"All right, Hume then," the Cardinal said. "If I remember rightly he ended up by doubting his own existence and that of the physical world as well. How can you expect people who are blind to the fact of earth to perceive the hint of heaven? To me the only answer seems to be an Infallible Church."

"And to me too, Your Eminence," the Archbishop said. "But you must admit that the Infallible Church has left a great many unconverted both in space and time. And I'm not so sure that the fault isn't largely our own. Have we honestly faced up to the intellectual difficulties which genuinely perplex our opponents? Surplus kittens having to be drowned at birth after having been so elaborately created by God. And the elaborately created cats eating the just as elaborately created mice and birds. Little girls born with their bladders between their legs."

"That's what Newman calls the 'aboriginal catastrophe'. Nature itself has fallen from grace, that's all."

"That doesn't help the rabbit caught in the gin trap," the Archbishop said. "And it's not much of an answer to give to a modern agnostic who wants to know whether Siamese twins will be resurrected joined together on the last day."

"The best we can do, Your Grace, is to quote Pascal and say that the heart has its reasons which reason knows not. And agnosticism isn't as modern as all that, either. Even Shakespeare speaks about falling into the dark cave of eternal light or something, doesn't he? What people don't seem to be able to understand is that there are other ways of apprehending God than talking about Him with one's mouth."

"Let's put it this way, shall we?" the Archbishop said. "Only two things will save the world: thought and prayer; and the trouble is that those who think don't pray and those who pray don't think."

"And that 75% of humanity is stupid and 75% wicked and that the other two 25%'s never coincide," the Cardinal said.

"And it'll take more than your Robert Hugh Benson to put that right, Your Eminence. I met a man on the train coming down yesterday, and do you know what he was reading? *The Garden of Allah*."

"That's nothing, Your Grace. You should try *Three Weeks*."

"Anyway, Your Eminence, this fish is excellent. Sent down by rail from Aberdeen, I expect?"

"No, Your Grace. Sent *up* by rail from Portsmouth."

6

" *Non clamor, sed amor, sonat in aure Dei*," the Archbishop said as he and Father Campbell stood at the back of the cathedral watching the beginning of the Capitular High Mass. " The straight line, the gentle fold, the clear prayer, that's what makes for devotion. But I wish His Eminence would stop those priests of his from smirking across the sanctuary at one another. What have any of us to grin about I wonder when we preach the truth so badly that it often sounds like lies ? "

7

" Anyway that makes one enemy of God less," a French priest said to Father Campbell after the auxiliary Bishop's funeral in Notre Dame next day. Father Campbell was shocked. The Mass of requiem sung by the Cardinal Archbishop of Paris had seemed to hold something of all the dirges that had ever been sung in the metropolitan cathedral, and he had been moved by the spectacle of the Archbishop of Inchkeith and the Pentlands sprinkling and censing the bier of his old friend the Bishop of Thermopylae.

" Oh, I grant you the silly old fool meant well," the French priest went on, " but that's not enough in France these days. Bishops ought to be more than walking bellies that suck up to atheist politicians at banquets. What do you imagine a working man in Belleville thinks of a Cardinal Archbishop of Paris who allows the Curé of St. Honoré d'Eylau to bless Boni de Castellane's new house in the Avenue du Bois? What do you imagine Boni thinks? Anyway I know what I think: and that is that His Eminence must be about as apostolically minded as Sarah Bernhardt's wooden leg. In the meantime my name's the Abbé Bonpapa and I've been ordered to take you to lunch while my Cardinal tells your Archbishop all he hasn't been doing to get Cleo de Mérode and Emilienne d'Alençon to make their Easter duties."

On their way to the restaurant it was still the Abbé who did the talking.

" For the special benefit of visiting British clergymen," the Abbé said with a grin as he pointed out an advertisement in English for the *Folies-Bergère*. " How right your George Moore was when he said that sexual morality in any given country at any given time was in inverse ratio to the height of the heels on women's shoes."

" But why does the municipality of Paris allow it? " Father Campbell asked.

" Because the municipality of Paris can't prevent it. Because the municipality of Paris doesn't want to prevent it. Because the Church in France, having, as Leo XIII rightly pointed out, lost the working classes, is now in the process of losing the upper and middle classes as well. Why else do you think Combes expelled the religious orders four years ago? Even Waldeck-Rousseau himself never intended to go as far as that."

"I suppose it all goes back to Voltaire," Father Campbell said.

"Say rather to Jean-Jacques Rousseau. Anyway as your Doctor Samuel Johnson said, 'it is difficult to settle the proportion of iniquity between them.' But the French clergy themselves are much more to blame. After our behaviour in the Dreyfus case it's surprising that they didn't throw out all us secular priests as well. But that's the Church of France all over. We preach justice and allow unbelievers like Zola and Clemenceau to practise it. Eldest Daughter of the Church indeed! Dried up old spinster's more like it. And now we've got what we deserve: Maurice Barrès in the Academy and Félix Faure at the Elysée. '*En France il y a deux pentes,*' I said in my sermon last Sunday, '*l'une vers Dieu, l'autre vers le diable. Tâchez de glisser dignement, mes bien chers frères,*' I said. 'It's the most we can do these days.' Well here we are, *Chez Théophraste.* I'm glad to see it's still open. Last week the waiters were on strike for the right to grow moustaches. And if that isn't schism, heresy, revolution and anarchy I'd like to know what is."

Most of the men with their napkins scowled at the sight of the Abbé Bonpapa's cassock; priests seemed even less popular in France than in Scotland, Father Campbell thought.

" *Caca d'oiseau sèche vite*," the Abbé said as he led Father Campbell to a vacant table next a young man reading *La Lanterne*. " They were as wrong as *La Croix* was about the Affaire but they've got to have a scapegoat and so it's us."

A moustacheless waiter handed them each a menu card and walked away again. Lunch with hors d'œuvre, eggs or fish or meat, dessert and wine was three francs, Father Campbell saw; with hors d'œuvre, eggs or fish, meat, dessert and wine three francs twenty-five; with hors d'œuvre, eggs, fish, meat, dessert and wine three francs fifty.

" I'm afraid it'll have to be the first lot of ' ors '," the Abbé said. " His Eminence only gave me eight francs and we've got to tip the waiter so that he can go on not growing a moustache with dignity now that he's got the right to grow it. Unless of course one of us were to order the fish and the other the meat and both have half a portion of each. They'd probably charge us a sou each for the extra plates but I think the Fund for the Construction of New Churches in the Parisian Suburbs could run to that."

The man at the next table lowered his paper.

" Why not let the Friends of Lay Education weigh in with another sou and then we could have a third of the three main dishes each ? " he asked.

Father Campbell was sorry when the Abbé Bonpapa

27

accepted: he was shy of meeting strangers and was only beginning to get used to the Abbé and would have liked to go on learning about the Church in France.

"My name is Armand Lucot," the young man said and threw at Father Campbell: "The strength of England is the uniformity of her mediocrity."

"That doesn't hold for Scotland," Father Campbell said coldly.

M. Lucot grinned.

"Of course it doesn't. Scotsmen are always welcome in France." He turned to the Abbé Bonpapa. "And now, Monsieur l'Abbé, what answers have you got to make to the nineteen shaky answers Ernest Renan says the Church gives."

"Twenty-four, Monsieur, you mean," the Abbé said.

"I warn you, Monsieur l'Abbé, I'm like Jean Messelier: I should like to see the last king strangled with the guts of the last priest."

"And I, Monsieur, should like to see the last Republican Socialist suffocated with the last apron of the last Freemason."

Soon Father Campbell was arguing too, and it was late in the afternoon when he got back to his hotel.

8

" We've got a bad press certainly," the Archbishop said when Father Campbell had told him about M. Lucot. " Generally we deserve it, but occasionally we don't. ' How can a bishop marry? ' Sydney Smith asked. ' How can he flirt? The most he can say is, " I will see you in the vestry after service ".' Catholic bishops can't even say that. Anyway there's this to be said for celibacy: the Church of God can't invite your sister-in-law to tea."

CHAPTER II

BUT IF the Church couldn't invite Father Campbell's sister-in-law to tea, it could send him to live in the same presbytery as Canon Samson-Slingsby, the thirty-two year old up-and-coming rector of East Hadwick. The son of wealthy parents, the Canon had had the choice of becoming a priest or of exporting soda water siphons to Roumania: God and the Archdiocese of Inchkeith and the Pentlands had won. He had, he said, a vocation for saving the souls of the rich and no Catholic Scot with a title ever got married without the Canon having a finger in the pie. While aware that the first should be last and the last first, he saw no reason why he should not be first at being

29

last, and if he was quite good at administering Extreme Unction to miners, he preferred playing golf with the Episcopal Bishop. Although he was still complaining of having been made to give Benediction three times on his first day as a curate at the pro-cathedral, he believed in putting his own curates through their paces from the beginning.

" I expect you're used to high tea," he said to Father Campbell as he helped himself to lamb cutlet on their first evening at dinner together. " Personally I can find nothing in any of the gospels which forbids a priest to live like a gentleman. On the contrary I sometimes think that Scotland would have been brought back to the Faith fifty years ago if it hadn't been for the six o'clock kippers swilled down with Mazawattee by Irish curates."

" That's all right, Canon," Father Campbell said. " It so happens I'm a convert."

" And what may I ask has the act of submission to the Holy See got to do with filling one's mouth with a sludge of scone and poached egg ? "

" Simply this, Canon." Father Campbell was now angry enough not to mind if he sounded conceited. " My home used to be Malhousie Castle."

The Canon looked impressed.

" Now I begin to understand. So that's why the Old Jock took you with him to Paris ! "

" No, I think it was because he was sorry for me—

none of my people turning up for my ordination and that sort of thing."

The Canon poured himself out some burgundy and pushed the decanter across to Father Campbell.

" Careful with it now. Don't swing it over your head like a dumbbell. It's a Clos Vougeot 1902."

A few sips of wine made Father Campbell feel a little more friendly towards his rector.

" There's one thing about His Grace," he said. " He never tries to come the great prelate."

" More fool him!" Canon Samson-Slingsby snorted. " I can tell you I'd come the great prelate all right if I were ever Archbishop of Inchkeith and the Pentlands. Just let me on the Old Jock's throne for three days and I'd show them a thing or two. Canon Poustie wouldn't go on holding his Bona Mors Society annual tea in the lounge of the Thistle, I can tell you. And another thing: I'd see that every priest in the Archdiocese had a sound knowledge of the secular philosophy he's got to condemn from the pulpit."

" I think that you're unjust to His Grace there, Canon. I can assure you that he's fully aware of that problem. You should have heard him talking to Cardinal Bourne about the necessity for answering David Hume when we were in London."

" Hume! Who wants to bother about him? It's this new chap Einstein who's coming along that we've got to answer. He says that it's wrong for physical scientists to interpret nature as a series of inevitable events of which the observer is no more than a witness. If that isn't one up the scholastics' kilts I'd very much like to know what is."

" I see."

" What do you see?"

" I mean that apart from the possibility of a miracle the physical scientists are perfectly right."

" Einstein doesn't say whether they are right or wrong," the Canon snapped. " What he is questioning is not the events themselves but whether the physical scientists' interpretation of them is practical. What he wants to know is whether we can separate inevitability from our observation of it. If we can't then he says we have no means of knowing that the physical world consists of the inevitable events themselves and not only of our observation of them. Therefore he says that the observer is a link between the event and its perception rather than a witness of it. It's going to be a job for the theologians to answer him, I can tell you. Strictly between ourselves I've started in already. *Freewill and the Molecule*, my little book's going to be called."

Father Campbell hoped he looked as respectful as he felt.

" This is the sort of subjective statement I've got to disapprove, Father. ' Everything is true; only the opposite is true; you must believe both equally or be damned.' "

" Did Einstein say that too, Canon? "

" Of course he didn't. I'm surprised at you, Father: a Campbell of Malhousie not recognising Robert Louis Stevenson when he hears him. Anyway I'm answering him as well. Then there's Comte and his assertion that there can be no assertion except that there can't be an assertion. I've got my work cut out, Father, I can tell you."

" I'm sure you have, Canon."

" So you see I've got two big activities in my life: the running of this parish and the writing of my book. Let's say a thousand souls in the parish and a couple of million readers of *Freewill and the Molecule*. And not only *quantitative* readers either, but *qualitative* readers who will influence the thinking of those around them."

Father Campbell thought he knew what was coming.

" So, Father, I'm counting on your understanding and help. On weekdays you'll say the six o'clock Mass at the convent and I'll say the eight o'clock here. In the mornings you give religious instruction in the school and in the afternoons you visit. ' Why didn't I see you at Mass on Sunday, Bridget?' is always a good opening gambit if people come to the door looking guilty. Then there's the prison. You've no idea how many good Kartholics get on the wrong side of Teddy Seven. Rosary and Benediction on Wednesdays and Fridays at eight and confessions

afterwards. Confessions again for the holy hens at
the convent on Thursdays too, but that oughtn't to
be a tax on your moral theology as Reverend Mother's
the only one who's likely to commit murder or rape.
On Saturdays there's the box again from five to
nine but I'll pop down about seven and give you a
hand. On Sundays the six at the convent and the
seven at the prison for you and I'll say the eight and
sing the eleven here. When you preach in the morning I'll spout in the evening, and *vice versa*. On
the whole I think that's a fair division of our apostolic labours." There wasn't a flicker of humour
on the self-important face. "And another thing,
Father, don't throw your slithers of used soap away.
I use them as stickers. If there's one thing I can't bear
it's waste."

2

Father Campbell however was anxious to exercise
his ministry and he set to work eagerly.

The first child he baptised was a baby girl born
without arms or legs. How right the Archbishop's
remarks to Cardinal Bourne had been, he thought as
he put salt on the small tongue and murmured
"*Accipe salem sapientiae*": it was almost impossible
to understand why God had not allowed this child to
die. The loophole that God was all-ruling rather than
all-powerful had been condemned on the ground that

omnipotence could not be mitigated. The traditional explanation that the suffering of the innocent could wipe out the cruelty of cads would satisfy only those who already loved God enough to trust Him.

That same afternoon he was called to two death-beds.

The Italian ice-cream merchant shouted "*Porco di Dio*" as soon as he caught sight of the priest's Roman collar. Father Campbell smacked his face, explained that final impenitence was the one sin which would certainly be punished with eternal deprivation, and just managed to wheedle him to approximate attrition before he died.

The Irishman, told to say "Jesus, mercy" when the crucifix was placed in his hands after he had been shriven and anointed, said "Jesus, Murphy" and went off happily, safe in the embrace of the Emerald Church.

On his return from the second death-bed Father Campbell found a note from Canon Samson-Slingsby, stating that he had been called out to explain indulgences to an Episcopalian marchioness, and asking him to instruct in his place a grocer's assistant who wanted to marry a Catholic laundress.

"What I want you to understand is this," he said to the raw face he found waiting in the parlour. "We're not going to ask you to become a Catholic unless we can manage to convince you that we are right; we've got quite enough bad ones on our hands as it is without wanting any more. As long as you really believe what your own Church teaches then you've a duty to remain where you are. *Subjectively* you're in good faith and that's all that matters in the eyes of God. But we believe that we are *objectively* right and that's why we insist on your children being brought up as Catholics and want you to understand at least a little about your future wife's religion."

" Aye."

It was all, Father Campbell said earnestly, a matter of authority. Once the Divinity of Christ had been accepted all the rest followed. If Christ was God He could neither deceive nor be deceived, nor could the Church which He Himself had said that he had founded on Peter. Hence the doctrines taught by that Church were mathematical truths as rigid as those of Euclid, no matter how grave the misconduct of those who had expounded them in the Middle Ages. By attempting to change dogma, Calvin, Knox and Cranmer had proved that they understood nothing at all about theology: one didn't try to keep an astronomer off chorus girls by forcing him to state that the sun revolved round the earth. One must not however confound dogma, which was unalterable, with matters of ecclesiastical discipline, such as fasting, abstinence and the celibacy of the clergy, which could be modified or abrogated as and when the Pope thought fit. A distinction must be made too between heresy and schism: the Greek Orthodox Church was chiefly schismatic and heretical only in its refusal to accept the primacy of Peter and the procession of the Holy Ghost from *both* the Father and the Son."

" And now," Father Campbell said when he had finished, " I hope you understand."

" Aye."

" All right. Just to make certain however perhaps you wouldn't mind telling me just what you do understand."

" Everything, Father. All yon aboot the Holy Spurrit being a Greek."

His experience of the confessional on Friday was scarcely more rewarding.

" Bless me, Father, for I have sinned," his first penitent said. " It's a week since my last confession. Since then I have made an indecent joke about lime juice—once. That's all I can remember, Father."

Even the Curé of Ars couldn't have started converting his parish on that.

His second penitent was a girl whose thoughts had wandered during her prayers, his third an old woman who had stolen a pound of sausages when the grocer wasn't looking and then put it back on top of the sugar bin, again when the grocer wasn't looking.

His fourth penitent demanded more skill. This sinner maintained that he was always in a state of grace because every time he " went with lassies " he made up his mind to go to confession immediately afterwards. The penitent was also concerned as to whether the pound which he had paid to a girl in the Thistle Hotel, twice, mattered more than the sixpence he had placed in a Salvation Army collecting box, once. A firm purpose of amendment, Father Campbell told him, was necessary to make any absolution valid, and an intention to repent, placed after an intention to sin, could scarcely be interpreted as that. Provided that the penitent's desire had not been to disseminate error but to promote charity, he thought that the penitent would have done better to put the two pounds in the Salvation Army collecting box and given threepence each time to the girl. Fornication was a sin, not only because it was pro-creative and it took twenty years to bring up a child, but because it obscured the vision of God and prevented an understanding of suffering.

By the time he reached his seventeenth penitent Father Campbell began to realise that his sinners had been at their lying and cheating and lusting and flinging haddocks at drunken husbands for quite a long time. He compelled himself to charity by telling himself that their perseverance in confessing the same faults Saturday after Saturday was at least indicative of their wish to be with God for ever, although why God should wish to be with them for ever was another matter. If heaven was not going to look like the second house of the Empire there would have to be glorified minds as well as glorified bodies.

A Thread of Scarlet

In spite of having recited his sermon five times in front of his bedroom mirror, Father Campbell had an attack of stage fright next morning at the eleven o'clock Mass while he waited for Canon Samson-Slingsby to finish reading out the list of Conversion of Scotland Sodality subscriptions from the foot of the altar steps:

"Mrs. Byrne, two shillings and sixpence; Mrs. Fearney, three shillings; Colonel Sir Anstruther Burt-Forbes, five pounds; Mrs. Skelly, sixpence. You'll have to do better than that next time, Mrs. Skelly: we won't get the clans galloping back to the Faith of their forefathers until we ourselves love God more than our second glass of beer."

"In the Name of the Father, and of the Son, and of the Holy Ghost. Amen," Father Campbell began. "'And there shall be one flock and one shepherd.'"

To begin with most of the congregation listened bravely enough but there were a good many eyes closed and rosaries clicking by the time he had got to: "I would ask you once and for all to rid yourself of the erroneous notion that the Eastern schism occurred under the Patriarchate of Photius in the last quarter of the ninth century. The real human cause of the rupture was the massacre of Western Christians by Greeks at Constantinople in 1182. A contributory cause was the conquest of Cyprus by Richard the First of England in 1191. Conversely the flames of hatred on the other side were fanned by the sack of

Constantinople in 1204 and the atrocities committed by French and Venetian adventurers and mercenaries." Only the conviction that the Canon at least must be appreciating his learning enabled him to carry on to his peroration: " In other words a desire to save their own skins made the Greeks salute the Prophet's turban rather than prostrate themselves before the Pope's tiara."

" Photius indeed! " the Canon barked at lunch as he poured out his second glass of wine. " Why not credit them with ' erroneous notions ' about the authorship of the *Anacreon* while you are about it? It's not courses in history these oafs require. It's hard stones flung at their bap faces about the Divinity of Christ and the four last things: death, judgment, heaven, hell. And your metaphors need watching too. From ' flames of hatred ' being ' fanned ' it's a short step to your ordering a couple of dozen ' doves of peace! ' "

Father Campbell could not even dull his shame with wine: the Clos Vougeot which had been shared on his first night was now drunk only by the Canon, who pencilled a Plimsoll line on the label of any unfinished bottle before he rose from table.

The silence of the nuns behind him when he said Mass at the convent next morning helped Father Campbell to recover his peace, and their strength was still with him when he visited the prison. Here the simple piety of many of the convicts amazed him and made him realise how close lay the impulses which separated the reprobate from the saint. Even the hardest nuts among the Irish had not been able to wipe off the dew which had fallen on Gideon's geographical fleece.

On the way out he met another clergyman coming in.

"My name is Arthur Pearson and I'm an ecclesiastic of the Anglican Disobedience," the parson said as he held out his hand with a friendly smile.

"Oh, I'd rather have a good Protestant than a bad Catholic any day of the week," Father Campbell said and hoped that he sounded convincing.

"I'm not so sure that I would," the Reverend Arthur Pearson said. "I'm not a fool. I know that Rome holds all the title deeds. But what worries me is the Infallibility of the Pope. Is it a sort of Dalai Lama business that takes place when a future Pope is conceived in his mother's womb and is kept gently on the boil until the Holiness immediately in front of him kicks the bucket and goes to his eternal reward?"

"It's more like a bulwark erected round the papal throne to keep the occupant from falling overboard." Father Campbell felt that it would be showing off to quote the decree of 1870. "In other words it's a hedge against error let down by the Holy Ghost."

"We're mixing our metaphors slightly, aren't we,

Father? Hedges aren't let down; they grow upwards."

"Let's call it an umbrella then, held above the head of each successor of St. Peter."

"Then why did Pius IX have to call an Oecumenical Council to decide whether the umbrella was there or not? Why didn't the Tridentine bishops notice it?"

"Probably because it was an invisible umbrella."

Both clergymen were still laughing at this when they parted.

When he sat down to prepare the sermon which would convince Canon Samson-Slingsby that he had convinced the bap faces that Christ was Divine, Father Campbell wished that he had some of his new friend's easy culture: he had missed Oxford through having gone straight to the Scots College immediately after his conversion. From Monday to Saturday he sought for a way of making the muddied words shine.

"Writers of comparative religion foolishly imagine that the similarity of false religions to Christianity prove that the true itself is false," he began when he got up into the pulpit on Sunday. "On the contrary it proves that the false religions are marginally true, because they are partial revelations of the full knowledge disclosed to us by Our Lord. The Egyptians believed in the resurrection of the dead, the Persians in the struggle between good and evil, the Chinese in honouring and obeying parents. All these doctrines Christ came down to earth to teach us and He summed up moral compulsion in two great commandments: to love God, with all our strength and our soul and our mind, and our neighbour as as ourselves. It is easy for us to love God, because Christ Himself was God. We know this because of the miracles He wrought when he was on earth and because of the miracles which He still works at Lourdes through the intercession of His Mother. We know it too because there were no more Jewish prophets after Him and because poetry ended with Malachi and began again with Matthew. It is not so easy for us to love our neighbour because his faults are generally so exact a reflection of our own that we can only hate him as we ought to hate ourselves; but however detestable he may appear to us we can always love him for the love of God. And among our neighbours must be counted the animals, as fearfully and wonderfully fashioned as we are."

"Not so dusty this time," the rector said as he pushed the Clos Vougeot across to Father Campbell at lunch. "But why all this sentimentality about animals? Dogs haven't got souls."

"Surely that's all the more reason for our being kind to them," Father Campbell said, trying to keep his voice from trembling. "I mean, as they aren't going to be compensated in an after life for cruelty done to them in this."

" I remember my *Summa* if you don't," Canon Samson-Slingsby said. " ' By divine providence, according to the law of nature, the animals are ordained for the use of man.' "

" For the *use* of man, Canon, not for his wanton cruelty."

" Will you kindly not interrupt me and St. Thomas of Aquin, Father. ' Therefore there is no injustice in man's using them either by killing them or in any other way.' ' *Vel quolibet alio modo*,' the Angelic Doctor's words are. And if that isn't one in the eye for the anti-vivisectionists, I don't know what is."

Father Campbell had to take a gulp of wine before he was able to reply:

" Cardinal Manning was an anti-vivisectionist. He said that nothing could justify such outrageous cruelty."

" Manning happens to have been a convert. Converts are always apt to slip back into the exercise of private judgment. On these matters I much prefer to take Father Rickaby as my authority." The Canon rose, went into his study, and came back with an open book from which he read out: " ' But there is no shadow of evil resting on the practice of causing pain to brutes *in sport*, where the pain is not the sport itself, but an incidental concomitant of it. Much more in all that conduces to the sustenance of man may we give pain to brutes, as also in the pursuit of science.

Nor are we bound to any anxious care to make the pain as little as may be. Brutes are *things* in our regard . . .'"

Father Campbell looked with horror at the rector's safe face. The cold cheeks, the loveless eyes, the untempted lips betrayed the executive who had indexed grace without ever having understood the need for mercy. Had the Canon's tenderness, he wondered, been entirely frozen by his celibacy? How would such a priest behave towards a woman run over in the street? Would he merely hear her confession? Could he ever be as brave about his own suffering as he was about that of animals? How would he stand up to having his starchy bowels howked out for the Trinity?

"Well," the Canon asked, "what have you got to say to that?"

"Simply this: if I were Pope I'd refuse the Sacraments to grouse shooters and big game hunters."

"Which just shows how badly you know your moral theology. If you'll take the trouble to look up Addison's and Arnold's Catholic Dictionary you'll find it in black and white that a man who puts animals to death in a cruel manner sins at worst venially—and that only because it's likely to make him cruel to his fellow men as well."

Father Campbell no longer required the Clos Vougeot to give him courage. For all the rector's quotations he knew that he was right and the Canon wrong. The umbrella over the Papal Throne had kept even Alexander VI and Julius II from being as heartless as the theologians.

"You can say what you like, Canon," he said, "but I'd rather have brothels in every town in Scotland than the Twelfth of August."

"I shall see that His Grace is informed of your preference, Father," Canon Samson-Slingsby said acidly.

3

The Archbishop sent for Father Campbell two days later.

"You're quite right, Father," he said. "One of the more impenetrable mysteries of the Faith is why lobsters should be boiled alive to feed Canons and not Canons lobsters. But to keep you from spiritual pride I'm going to quote St. Augustine to you: 'These also my heart hated, though not with a perfect hatred: for perchance I hated them more because I was to suffer by them, than because they did things utterly unlawful.' Are you sure that it's because he's hard on animals and not because he's hard on you that you're having all this trouble with Canon Samson-Slingsby?"

"I hope so, Your Grace."

"Then the only thing you've got to do is to offer him up. Before you can hope to make others try to be saints you've got to try to be one yourself. And now that priests are no longer hanged, drawn and quartered at Tyburn one of the few means to sanctity still at their disposition is putting up with their fellow priests. The pain mayn't be quite so acute but it lasts longer. Just think of how the Curé of Ars bore with the Abbé Monnet."

"Tolerating our fellow priests won't help animals, Your Grace," Father Campbell said.

"No theologian has ever solved that problem," the Archbishop said. "Even Catholic Dukes are more interested in the speckle on a trout than in the radiance of Cherubim and Seraphim. And Our Lord Himself told the Apostles to let down their nets. Even the anchorites seem to have abstained from flesh meat more to deprive themselves of pleasure than to save animals from pain. Probably that too is all part of Newman's 'aboriginal catastrophe.'"

"But that doesn't excuse Canon Samson-Slingsby from ignoring suffering, Your Grace."

"The trouble with the Canon is that he always lives down to his reputation. But if you want to become a good priest, Father, you must empty yourself of yourself."

"But it's not myself I'm worrying about, Your Grace. It's the animals. I just can't be happy when I think of the cruel things people do to them."

"You're not meant to be, Father." The Archbishop took Father Campbell by the arm and led him up to look at a photograph on the wall. "That's me at Blair's in 1852," he said pointing to a faded seminarian in a yellowish brown group. "When you want to spot the future bishop look for the dunce."

CHAPTER III

"MAN, YOU'RE a picture," the Archbishop said when Father Campbell came to say good-bye in 1916 before joining his unit. "What a pity chaplains can't wear the kilt. Come over to the light now so that I can have a good look at you." He dragged the priest over to the window. "There's two things people can never understand from outside: the British Empire and the Catholic Church. How lucky we are to belong to both of them, and how sorry other folk are for us."

A cinema theatre named the Threepenny Scratcher had now been opened next the Thistle Hotel, up whose steps a girl in high boots and a fur-trimmed bell-bottomed coat was swinging on the arm of a Royal Scots officer.

"More raw material for me, I shouldn't wonder," the Archbishop said. With two of the cathedral curates away at the war, the Archbishop had been taking his turn in the confessional; he was getting deaf, however, and at least one of his admonitions

48

was rumoured to have been overheard: "Was she pretty? Then there was no excuse. The seven penitential psalms on your knees every night for a week."

"No matter how bad they become, Father," the Archbishop went on, "always try to get them to stay on in the Church and let themselves be looked after from within rather than from without. And don't be too hard on the *recidivi* either. There's a story about a Spanish priest refusing absolution and the figure on the crucifix freeing an arm to bless the penitent and saying to the priest: 'I shed My Blood for him; you didn't.'"

The girl and the officer had gone now, and the new notice on the left of the porch was uncovered again:

THE THISTLE HOTEL

WHERE YOU COME

FOR

A LARK

"I only hope that we come out of this war with as clean hands as we went into it," the Archbishop said. "Christians oughtn't to need armies and navies to protect them from other Christians; but I suppose one's got to be a bit of a St. Vincent de Paul to love two thousand million neighbours as oneself. Sometimes when I see all this muddle around us I am tempted to think that the vast careers of our certitudes revolve round doubt after all. But perhaps we're not meant

D

to know the truth. Perhaps all we're intended to do is to live decently and then be rewarded by the felicity in which we have not quite been able to believe."

Father Campbell hoped he looked as though he understood. Was he never going to get away from having to listen to his superiors talking philosophy?

" As Cardinal Bourne said, Your Grace, faith has to have merit."

The Archbishop did not seem to have heard. He walked to the other window and stood looking out at the hills, burning in the sunset like a row of lighted Christmas puddings.

" Anyway," he said as he turned, " the apparatus hasn't yet quite killed the spirit, and the mark can still be seen through the muck. Who knows? Perhaps we've still a chance of stopping the Gadarene rush before the politicians reach the edge of the cliff."

2

Lieutenant-Colonel G. M. S. Pollock-Buchan looked round with a scowl when Father Campbell entered the Battalion Orderly Room, and then went on talking to the Regimental Sergeant-Major:

" In future the scabbard as well as the bayonet itself must be polished. And the C.S.M. of Don Company must be ticked off about that shocking at-the-halt-on-the-left forming platoon. Beer Company to be put through SS.134 until it becomes second nature to the brutes. All right. Carry on, Sergeant-Major."

The R.S.M. saluted, banged dust out of the floor boards with his feet, about-turned and stamped out.

" Well ? "

Father Campbell did his best to imitate the R.S.M.'s salute.

" I'm the new priest," he said.

" R.C. padres we call 'em. Anyway I don't know what they've sent you here for. Most of the men are Presbyterian or United Board and the officers are C. of E.—when they remember. Still no doubt you'll come in handy enough when we're in the line, dishing out cigarettes and things. In the meantime what I want you to get into your head is this: my men are in the army to fight and I'm not very concerned about how often they forget to say their prayers before they go to bed at night so long as they get up in the morning full of hatred for Huns. As long as you remember that you and I ought to rub along together all right. I'm presuming of course that like most R.C.'s you drink like a fish."

" Let's say like a sardine."

" ' Like a sardine, *sir*,' you mean. You don't call your bishop wallah ' old cock ', do you ? "

" Like a sardine, *sir*."

" Then you'd better pray to bloody Jonah and get him to turn the sardine into a whale. All right.

Carry on. Dinner's at seven. We generally get blotto in the ante-room first."

Father Campbell saluted the stupid, malignant face and marched out, despising himself for having been weak from motives of human respect. Of one thing he was certain: for all his non-practising Anglicanism, Lieutenant-Colonel Pollock-Buchan would never have dared to speak to the Old Jock like that.

To atone for his cowardice he went to the ante-room at half-past six and sat down and opened the *Catholic Trumpet*, turning the front page with its dreadful headlines outwards: BLACKPOOL NUN SPANKED FUTURE BISHOP; CATHOLIC WATCHDOG PRAISED BY BAPTIST MAYOR.

"Well, Paton," he heard the C.O. ask, "and how did you spend your leave? Women, I suppose?"

"No, sir."

"Booze then?"

"No, sir."

"Then what the hell did you do with yourself?"

"I played golf, sir."

"Hear that, Wedderburn? He says he played golf—the bloody liar."

"Education in the Christian tradition marks every man who receives it with a respect for, if not an understanding of, the timeless human value of holy purity," Father Campbell read and looked up to see that the *Bystander* in the next chair had been lowered.

"Good evening, Father. My name's Inches. I

expect you're finding things a little bit strange at first." The face was friendly, and devoid of the cautious expression assumed by most laymen when talking to a priest.

" Are you a Catholic?" Father Campbell asked.

" ' Was ' I suppose would be more correct."

Father Campbell was shocked. So far he had dealt only with penultimate apostates terrified into attrition by the approach of death.

" What's the matter?" he asked warily: a woman, his professors had taught him, would generally be found behind every so-called intellectual difficulty.

" What's not? The whole Holy Catholic, Apostolic and Roman Church has proved herself a washout, that's all."

His professors had prepared Father Campbell for this statement too.

" Churchmen perhaps, but not the Church," he said primly.

" You can't get out of it by playing with words, Father. The Church is the Assembly of the Faithful, isn't it? And they've all sold out to the enemy from Pope Benedict XV to the godparents of the last brat baptised in Balbao."

" I think that's a slight exaggeration, Captain."

" I'm ' Captain ' only with ' Inches ' attached. Only field officers and above are addressed by their rank without their name."

" Thank you, Captain Inches."

53

" Inches to you."

" Thank you, Inches, then. What you seem to be forgetting are the unknown saints." Father Campbell thought of Irish housemaids emptying chamber pots to the greater glory of God. " The Church buries hundreds of them every day and every day more hundreds grope to take their place."

" Perhaps. But it's known saints, not unknown ones, that the world needs just now. Saints people can take a look at. Saints as visible as the Bing Boys on Broadway. Saints as big as Clemenceau and Lloyd George and Horatio Bottomley. And instead what does the Church give us? French and German Bishops cutting one another at a Conclave. A Pope who condemns atrocities in the guarded terms of a Delphic oracle with laryngitis. Did Christ tell us to turn the other cheek or didn't he?"

" The Church has always taught that war was justifiable in self-defence."

" Both gallant little Belgium and Germany can't be defending themselves, can they?"

" They can both *think* they are."

" Trying to bring the lost sheep back, padre?" the C.O. shouted across the room and raised his glass. " Good luck to you anyway. All the same I must say I think it was pretty unsporting of the Deity to have put all those bits of fluff into the world and then mat a chap because he likes living *à la carte*."

Had there after all been excessive propping of the

54

bourgeois moralities, Father Campbell wondered at
dinner while Lieutenant-Colonel Pollock-Buchan was
telling them what King Edward VII had said when
he had looked down the barrel of Private McIlwraith's
dirty rifle at the Royal Inspection in Kirriemuir in
1903. Had the Archbishop been even more right
than His Grace had imagined, and was the Form now
entirely emptied of Spirit? The Reformation had
been caused by bad bishops and bishops could be bad
again now: prelates were notoriously better at un-
learning than learning. The Old Jock had admitted
his dislike of war, but even he hadn't spoken out and
condemned it. How far had the Archbishop's
reticence been prompted by an honest conviction
that Britain was right and Germany wrong?

Afraid that his silence might be taken for rudeness,
Father Campbell turned to the pig-faced subaltern on
his right.

"Have you been here long?" he asked.

"Long enough to get fed to the teeth. Blighty's
no boon as far as I'm concerned."

Father Campbell tried to sound manly:

"Want to go back and have another crack at the
enemy, that it?"

"Another crack at the girls in Rouen's more like
it, padre," the subaltern on Father Campbell's left
said.

Father Campbell did his best to smile broad-
mindedly.

"You've been reading the newspapers too much, padre," the pig-faced subaltern said. "It's not King and Country I'm fighting for out there. It's for my own bloody life. And the poor sods on the other side are fighting for their lives too."

A coarse remark from the other end of the table sent Father Campbell back to unhappy silence. So far he had dealt with sex and sin only in the academic atmosphere of approximate repentance. This was like seeing the vivisectionist pluck the cat's eyes out instead of only reading about it.

He was glad to escape for a walk through the lines with Captain Inches.

"Well, what do you think of our crusaders, Father? Not exactly fired with zeal for righteousness, are they? But what else can you expect when the only target you set them is not getting into bed with pretty girls they aren't married to?"

"Chastity is an essential condition of piety," Father Campbell said coldly.

"Is it? I thought it was an evangelical counsel. Intended only for priests and monks and nuns. But that's not the point. The point is you aren't asking people to set their sights high enough. If the Hierarchy were to get up in a body and tell them that it is more un-Christian to blow out a German boy of nineteen's guts in a dug-out because you can't be bothered taking prisoners than to pick up a tart on Piccadilly you'd be surprised how many chaps

56

would listen. Why I might even come crawling back myself."

" Individual bishops and priests may have failed." Father Campbell tried to vary the words of the rest of the apologetic so as not to sound too pat. " But the very fact that you are able to tell me they have failed is a proof that the Church itself has not. It's because the Church has kept the gospel message intact that you can apply Christ's teaching as a standard."

A fatigue squad came sliding along between the huts. " 'Eft, 'eft, 'eft, 'oight, 'eft,'' a corporal was shouting at them. " Eyes—'oight ! '' Captain Inches answered the salute.

" Conchies," he explained. " And not one Catholic among them. Doesn't that put us to shame? Heretics and schismatics having the courage to stand up for Christ's teaching and Father Bernard Vaughan on top of a tank selling War Bonds ! ''

He was off again before Father Campbell could think of a reply:

" I saw how shocked and surprised you were by the conversation in the Mess to-night. But why should you have been? How can you expect those you encourage to break God's greatest commandment to boggle at the lesser ones? How can you expect those who are taught to hate not to kick over the touchline occasionally in their loving ? ''

" You'll be saying next that it's this uniform you

and I are wearing that I ought to be shocked by," Father Campbell said bitterly.

"I'm not so sure that it isn't. And it's not only in time of war that the Church goes wrong either. It's in peacetime too. Why all this noise about hobble skirts and not a word about industrialists who make a fortune out of their workmen by underpaying them? Why do you gabble over the coffins of the poor and bury the rich old bitch with pomp? Why does the Cardinal marry the brewer and the curate the dustman? Where does Our Lord come into all that? If the Church is Christ's Bride He must be weeping over her as He did over Jerusalem?"

"I think you are wrong to imagine that there aren't Churchmen who are just as concerned as you are about these things. My own Archbishop, I assure you . . ."

Captain Inches interrupted Father Campbell so that they could watch the conscientious objectors being fallen out under the sneering eyes of the fighters.

"No, Tom," a gaunt man said as he passed with a comrade. "In Two Chronicles Eight Seventeen it says quite distinctly that Solomon went to both Eziongeber and to Elioth."

"How does that square with talk about chorus girls putting their knickers in their handbags?" Captain Inches asked.

CHAPTER IV

THE BATTALION went to France late in 1917, and
Father Campbell was surprised to find the front turn
out to be small enough for him to run into the Abbé
Bonpapa, saying Mass as a soldier priest at the next
altar to his in a village church. They breakfasted
together on the terrace of a café afterwards. Outside
the wine shop next door a Major in a British warm
was making up to a girl leaning against a barrel.

" *Pour l'Anglais le sexe commence à Calais*," the Abbé
said. "However even the clergy play when they get
away from the cat. The other day I walked into a
presbytery and found two monks rolling corks at
bottles. The Benedictine who hit the bottle got the
Benedictine. Perhaps they were celebrating their
good fortune in having been spared marriage with a
Christian woman."

" And Monsieur Armand Lucot ? " Father Campbell
asked, not sure whether the Abbé was joking or not.

" He's a *député* now, but he's not like a lot of the
others: driving cars for generals in the Loire. He's
in the front line and he's been very brave—unfortunately for us. After the war he'll be able to say
it wasn't only the Catholics who did the fighting.

All the friars and monks who were kicked out in 1903 are back in the trenches, but Monsieur le Conseiller d'Etat Armand Lucot may be able to prevent us getting credit even for that. Mark my words, he'll go right up top, and poor France will be back again where she started—in the lake. And we'll have only ourselves to thank: Henri Barbusse is telling the truth about the war, the Bishops aren't."

Watching the Abbé at the altar, with his pale blue puttees sticking out under his alb, Father Campbell had thought that, in the double anonymity of soldier and priest, he had at last seen the rendering unto God and unto Cæsar. Had the image and superscription been only Mammon's after all? The Abbé's views confirmed his own. No British soldier he had ever met had talked like a *Continental Daily Mail* Leader, and Don Quixotes had been as rare as Old Bills.

" ' Ninon was a naught-ee girl,' " the Major quoted as he prodded the arched stomach with his swagger cane.

"It's paradoxical," the Abbé went on, "but as far as I can see our only hope lies in the eradicable stupidity of our *bourgeoisie*. Voltaire doesn't cut much ice with a grocer's wife who wants to see her small daughter process into church in a pretty white veil, and just possibly the child's first communion may not be her last."

"You're lucky," Father Campbell said. " In Britain we haven't even got tradition to help us:

with us belief in God will soon be like belief in the devil—a superstition."

"'*La plus belle ruse du diable est de nous persuader qu'il n'existe pas.*'" Even above his scruffy uniform the Abbé's sore face still looked a priest's.

"All the same God can't have been such a bad economist as to invent the complicated mechanism of the Atonement solely in order to save saints."

"St. Augustine didn't seem to think so," the Abbé said and quoted: 'Love alone then is the stamp which marks out the sons of God from the sons of Satan. Anybody can make the sign of the cross and say amen and shout alleluia. Anybody can get baptised, go to church and build basilicas. It is still only by their love that you can tell those who are born of God. Love is the mighty mark, the indispensable franking. Lack it and have all the other virtues and you're still not through. Lack all the rest and have that one and you've fulfilled the law.' Perhaps more than we imagine will get in that way."

"I like to think so. Anyway it's our chief British virtue: loving our neighbour."

"So it would seem," the Abbé said with an amused glance at the Major who was now asking the one question he was likely to know in French.

"All the same there's a danger of humanism there, isn't there?" Father Campbell said, remembering what the Archbishop had said about the Form and the Spirit.

When it was time for them to part they still hadn't got the matter settled.

"*L'Eglise trépidante*," the Abbé said as he jumped on his bicycle and rocked the front wheel slowly. "The Church wobbles, but it never quite falls over."

2

"I've news for you," Lieutenant-Colonel Pollock-Buchan barked at Father Campbell when the priest entered the ante-room on his return to Battalion Headquarters. "We've been ordered up to the line and your friend Captain Inches has just told me that he refuses to lead his Company into the trenches. He says now that the Russians have thrown in their hands, we've no longer any excuse for going on. I want you to go and tell him with all your priestly authority that that sort of nonsense doesn't cut any ice with me and that if he doesn't parade with Beer Company at five pip emma tonight I'll have him put under close arrest and charged with desertion in the face of the enemy."

3

Father Campbell was unsuccessful : Captain Inches maintained that for him cowardice would be to brave the many bullets which might not kill him and to funk the one which certainly would. What had happened in Russia, he said, was the beginning of real witness for the people, and if martyrs were required to awaken misled British soldiers to the same revolt he was willing to lead the way. What he would not do was to kill German soldiers who had done him no harm.

Lieutenant-Colonel Pollock-Buchan was as good as his word: Captain Inches was placed under close arrest, courtmartialled when the Battalion came out of the line and condemned to death. The findings and the sentence were confirmed by the Commander-in-Chief. The day before Captain Inches was due to be shot Father Campbell went in desperation to Divisional Headquarters to put in a last-minute plea for mercy through the Senior Chaplain.

" My dear fellow, the fellow must be mad," the Anglican said when Father Campbell told him what he had come about. " Just look at all the atrocities the Hun has committed. If that doesn't make the war a righteous one I'd very much like to know what does."

" Are you so sure the atrocities are all on one side ? " Father Campbell asked, remembering what Captain Inches had told him about British troops being ordered to finish off unwanted German prisoners. " And such comparative decency as we happen to have, doesn't it boil down to mere good form ? "

" And what else is good form but Christianity without the prayers ? "

" I very much wonder. Good form scarcely squares up with Pascal's definition of religion as betting one's whole life on the existence of God."

" Don't worry, Father. Take it from me: the Church's great opportunity is going to come *after* the war. The men aren't going to forget the brother-hood they learned out here in the trenches. Not on your life they aren't! And brotherhood's Christianity even if good form isn't. If you don't believe me you've only got to go round the dug-outs and listen to the way the chaps talk to one another when the shells are coming over."

" St. James did not say ' Let your yea be F. yea and your nay F. nay'."

" F. means very," the Senior Chaplain said.

" Anyway the longer I stay out here the more I'm inclined to agree with Captain Inches when he says that if there's one sort of war we aren't fighting it's a Christian one. Your bishops and mine are talking through their mitres when they say that we're fighting for the Sermon on the Mount. We're fighting so that the same cads and their sons and their sons' sons can still be seen in the Royal Enclosure at Ascot."

" Don't say that to the Corps Commander whatever you do. He's the best bet if you want to get your friend off. I'll run you over in the bus. There's just a chance that he may be helpful; but he certainly won't be if you insist on telling him that fox-hunting wasn't invented by the Apostles. He's a staunch Protestant who'll do anything for his religion except go to church for it, and he regards prayer as a redundant salute to sidereal emptiness."

"Well, old man, what do you say?" came in classic English through the Senior Chaplain's open window. "Do we——before we dine, or do we dine before we——?"

"Still think it means very?" Father Campbell asked.

4

They found Lieutenant-General Sir Brian Darkly-Cummerledge-Darkly, K.C.B., seated under a row of Kirchner girls showing knickers like meringues.

"Stuffy Buffy copped it yesterday," he told the Senior Chaplain. "Had to have his leg chopped off at the C.C.S. And it can't be sent up to heaven marked ' TO BE CALLED FOR ' either because it's been burned. Now don't tell me that doesn't stymie resurrection because it jolly well ought to. Now what can I do *you* for?" he asked Father Campbell. "If it's for the Pope to visit the trenches it'll have to be the week after next because I've got a Mormon delegation from Salt Lake City arriving on Monday."

"It's about Captain Inches, sir," Father Campbell said.

The Corps Commander's good humour vanished.

"Nothing doing. When privates are shot for cowardice I can't let an officer off. Inches funked it and now he's got to pay the price."

"He didn't funk it, sir. Captain Inches doesn't believe that this war's being fought for righteousness, that's all."

"Nor do I. Nor does anybody in his senses. What next!"

"Captain Inches also thinks that it's wrong to use force as a means of political persuasion, sir. He's sincere, sir. He thinks that the British and the French and the German soldiers ought all to throw down their arms like the Russians have."

"Then he's a fool as well as a coward. What else are Lenin and Kerensky doing but using force as a means of political persuasion? And you, padre, ought to know that better than anybody. What about all those priests who've been chucked into the Neva and left to drown under the ice? In any case all that was gone into at the courtmartial. Inches's argument just won't wash. If you want my honest opinion it's just a bit of camouflage to hide his wind-up at the idea of having to go over the top."

"I think you're wrong about that, sir. I knew

him at the Depot in Scotland. He was saying the
same sort of thing then."

" All that proves is that he had the wind-up well
in advance."

But Father Campbell had seen worldly faces like
the General's in his father's billiard-room and he
knew that kindness could lie behind them.

" Supposing *I* can get Captain Inches to see reason,
sir ? " he pleaded. " Who knows ? Even yet I might
get him to change his mind."

" You'd still have to persuade the Commander-
in-Chief to change his. Sorry, padre, but it's too
late now. Inches is for the high jump at six ack
emma tomorrow, and there is nothing I can do
about it."

" There is, sir. You can get through on the
telephone to the Commander-in-Chief and ask him
to give Inches one last chance." In case he should
see the General's face hardening Father Campbell
looked out of the window and threw his despair at
the black leafless arms of the supplicating trees.

" What do you think, Harrington ? Not another
word out of you, Father. I want the Book of Common
Prayer to speak for itself without any promptings
from blasphemous fables fondly imagined."

" I think the same as Father Campbell, sir, otherwise
I shouldn't be here."

" All right. I'll put it up to the Commander-in-
Chief. Don't thank me yet, Father," the General

snapped as he reached for the telephone. "The answer may still be a lemon."

The Commander-in-Chief was not at G.H.Q.

"Better stay to dinner both of you," the General said.

It was midnight before the Commander-in-Chief returned and the General got through to him.

"Worked it, by Jove," the General said when he came back from the telephone. "If Captain Inches will drop his nonsense the G.O.C. will quash the sentence. Instead Inches will be reduced to the ranks and sent over the top at the hottest part of the line as a private. The Old Boy's ordered the M.P.'s to wait till seven."

It was still dark when Father Campbell drove up at the gates of the military prison in Béthune.

"Come with the opium pellet, have you?" Captain Inches sneered. "Well, you can put it where the monkey put the nuts."

"You've got it all wrong about the Russians," Father Campbell said. "They're as bad as anybody else." Then he informed Captain Inches of the Commander-in-Chief's conditions.

"Tell him from me he can take a running jump at himself." Through the window bars came the indolent obscenity of parodied Colonel Bogey. "'And he hath put a new song in my mouth, even praise unto our God,'" Captain Inches quoted derisively.

Father Campbell remembered that it was only by losing his temper that he had managed to pull in the dying Italian in East Hadwick.

" And why do you think there are contemplatives in the world? " he shouted. " What are the *Magnificats* for if it isn't to drown the *Bollocky Bills*? Why do Carmelites live in damp cells and pray from morning to night but never for themselves? To atone for the cruelties and bestialities you imagine you can stop by your dramatics. To storm God into making stiff-necked fools like you see sense. You mayn't under-stand the arithmetic of it, but the lives of the saints have proved that God does."

Captain Inches did not answer, and Father Campbell went on:

" What's the matter with you is superficiality. The Church isn't just High Mass and incense floating above altars. The Church is an absolute in which we see reflected our own approximations. And only a madman could imagine that Bolsheviks who murder priests and nuns can get people to lead better lives than she can. Britain may not know it but she is fighting for God's cause, which is equity and justice among the peoples of the world. I admit that German and Austrian bishops think the opposite, but then the Holy Ghost wasn't sent to protect prelates from *political* error. Would even a drunken Highland Light Infantryman throw a Greek patriarch into a frozen river? You know perfectly well that he wouldn't, and even this negative charity will excuse his mostly well-meant heresies. Another thing: for the moment you're too near the battle to see the aim for the smoke. But when it's all over you'll be proud of the new world you helped to make. Even Catholics will be Christians again. You'll see."

Somehow the jumble of false premises and un-distributed middles worked. That afternoon Captain Inches was stripped of his badges of rank in front of the battalion and sent as a private to the 51st Division.

CHAPTER V

DYING IRISHMEN in East Hadwick were still saying "Jesus, Murphy" when Father Campbell was made rector in 1926 and Canon Samson-Slingsby promoted administrator of the pro-cathedral and Vicar-General of the Archdiocese. Canon Samson-Slingsby had now become Monsignor Canon Samson-Slingsby and the Threepenny Scratcher the Sixpenny Scratcher.

On the Vigil of Pentecost, irritated by a penitent's comparison of temptations with bunkers on a golf course, Father Campbell barked through the grille:

"Well, you can always try to go round in as few strokes as possible, can't you?"

"What's bogey, Father?"

" Bogey's none."

He was ashamed of his impatience as soon as his penitent had gone: even the temporarily contrite had the one great merit of daring to be written off as hypocrites by those who were never sorry, and inconsistency consistently pursued might very well be one of the roads to sanctity.

His irritation returned when his next penitent accused himself of not always appreciating his wife properly when he woke up in the morning.

When was he going to hear somebody accuse himself of things he hadn't done, Father Campbell wondered as he half-listened on. Although there were few Catholics in Scotland rich enough to be mean, some at least must have underpaid those who worked for them. The sins he was told were generally as imperfect as the sorrow expressed for them. Most of the faithful seemed to bet on both horses: they drank and went with women in case whisky and girls might turn out to be all there was, and tried to repent afterwards in case they had guessed wrongly. How many believed with understanding? Five out of every thousand? No wonder the apologists were always scratching away. Perhaps that was why they wrote so badly. And how many would be saved? One in ten, the Archbishop had said. Ninety per cent down the ages must make quite a crowd in hell. One thing, however, was certain: you'd be able to recognise your friends and acquaintances as soon as you got there. Hell wouldn't only be the Absence; it would also be very much the presence.

"Try to remember that you may get on your wife's nerves as much as she gets on yours. For your penance say One Hail Mary." Was this teaching all nations to observe all things whatsoever He had commanded? Father Campbell didn't think so.

"Bless me, Father, for *you* have sinned. It's nine years since my last confession and I have no intention of making another. Where is that new Christian world you sent me to fight for? The lies you told me at Béthune have all come false."

Even if Father Campbell had not known the voice there was no mistaking the phraseology. He asked Captain Inches to leave the confessional and follow him into the sacristy. He heard the tap of a stick behind him in the aisle but it wasn't until he turned and saw the black glasses and the silver G.R.I. discharge badge and that the stick was white that he realised that his old friend was blind.

"My poor chap," he said, "I had no idea. Why did you never tell me?" Father Campbell was shocked, and more shocked still to discover that part of his horror was for his own predicament. He was almost glad when Captain Inches went on with his reproaches:

"Was the General Strike the brotherly love you prophesied? Is *No, No, Nanette* another way of singing the *Nunc Dimittis*? Is Mussolini's Italy God's

Kingdom on Earth? Is this mess why Argyll and Sutherland Highlanders were machine-gunned on the barbed wire? Were Gordons burned to death by flame-throwers so that Gentlemen might Prefer Blondes and Sir Edmund Gosse warn us against the danger of praising Elizabethan literature excessively?"

"Perhaps it wasn't all as useless as you make it sound. There are other things, too." Father Campbell decided not to mention the law of mystical substitution: to tell a blind man to unite and offer his suffering with Christ's a priest would require to be blind himself.

"I know. Each time some careless old cow bumps into me in the street there's going to be whoopee in heaven because my not swearing has made a Brazilian coffee planter stop sending roses to his mistress." The two shining black pennies were fixed on Father Campbell with the relentless accuracy of the sightless. "That it, eh?"

"I can't explain," Father Campbell said. "Suffering is God's law, that's all. It's a mystery."

"Like the Carmelites and the contemplatives you told me about in Béthune. Well, I'm fed up with mysteries. And so's the rest of the thinking world as far as I can gather. People want a straight answer nowadays. If you ever stumble across one you'll find me at the Salvation Army Hostel. They at least practise what they preach."

Father Campbell accompanied Captain Inches to the door of the church, and stood watching the shabby figure work its way along the pavement past girls in summer frocks. He tried to get rid of his guilt by telling himself that if Inches had been shot by the firing squad with hatred in his heart he would have lost God for ever. But how was he going to make Captain Inches understand that in his present mood? The Archbishop had been right in what he had said to Cardinal Bourne. Where was the metaphysician who could persuade the blind and the poor that their misery, if supernaturally accepted, washed the world like Keats's moving waters or a Benedictine *Salve*?

He was preaching to himself as well when he told his congregation next day that priests were necessary, not only to carry God's message to man, but also to get a reply out of man to carry back to God. Nobody looked very interested, and Father Campbell got down from the pulpit discouraged. How would the loyalty of such dolts stand up to persecution if it came? How would the Mass-misser behave on the rack?

He was back at metaphysics again as soon as he sat down on the sedilia, waiting for the choir to finish the *Credo*. Why had God made the world appear just as it would have done if religion hadn't been true? Why was it His will that philosophers should go on banging their heads against a roofless sky? Was the power of religion to make people good intended to prove that the merciless avoirdupois of the universe wasn't reality? Did the hint of gentleness behind oust the cold basic fear? Was the truth made known only to those who desired to love God? Was that why Catholics were allowed to be so brainless? With so many taking the geometric gases of the galaxies for Alpha and Omega, was the liquefaction of the blood of St. Januarius every 19th of September in Naples enough? A series of uncontrovertible little miracles of mercy would have made even the most hostile realise that religion was something more than a poetic interpretation of geology.

Next afternoon when he went to the convent he found two queues of nuns: one outside his confessional, and the other outside the parlour for the dentist. Molars and venial sins ran neck and neck until Sister Gertrude's decay in her left incisor was charted before her impatience with Sister Juliana was forgiven, but the dentist waited to examine Father Campbell's mouth too when he came out of the box.

" That eye tooth of yours is a bit wobbly," the dentist said. " Three years I give it. Ten if you'll let me make a bridge."

" Thanks; no foreign bodies in my mouth for me," Father Campbell said and ran to catch the train for his appointment with the Archbishop.

2

" Father Macpherson's with the Old Jock for the moment," Monsignor Samson-Slingsby told Father

Campbell when he arrived at the clergy house. "Moaning about being sent into the Old Priests' Home at Glenlady. If he were in my shoes he'd be only too glad to be offered the chance of a rest. No breakfast till noon to-day because I had to sing the requiem for Colonel O'Shaughnessy and paddle out to the cemetery as well. Anyway I had a good hot bath first. And would you believe it? The Old Jock still isn't washing himself with the ends of the bath soap before using the top and the bottom. How on earth he expects me to stick a big bit on a small bit afterwards beats me."

A marmalade cat which had been washing itself under the table jumped upon Father Campbell's knee.

"He'll cover you with hairs," the Vicar-General said. "He's ruined a cassock for me already. And do you think the Old Jock cares? Not he. Tartan Tom, he calls the beast. Found him starving outside the Thistle, he says. In his place I'd have let him starve."

"The Archbishop happens to be a Christian, Monsignor." Now that he was rector of a parish on his own Father Campbell was less afraid of the Vicar-General.

"Being a Christian doesn't mean he's got to be a mug. You've no idea the pitching in he gave me when he caught me tearing up a Converts' Aid Society Appeal the other day. And do you know his latest?

76

There's to be an Archdiocesan pilgrimage to Lourdes and he's given me the job of organising a bazaar and a Lucky Dip for those who can't afford the fare. Another little leg up with *Freewill and the Molecule*! Unfortunately Canon Law won't allow us to borrow the bearded woman from the Carnival but the Episcopal Dean's lending me a roulette table which he says has got a wonderful brake. Of course it's not as though I were going to be dishonest."

"Just cheat a little, that all, Monsignor?" The Archbishop was standing in the doorway in his old cassock with the faded purple sash. "However as I am exceedingly anxious that you should save your soul you will perhaps be kind enough to ring up the Dean and tell him that we shall not require his machine."

Without waiting for the Vicar-General to reply, the Archbishop took Father Campbell by the arm and led him along the passage to his study.

"One of the saddest things that one learns as a priest is how seldom the professionally noble can be trusted to behave with ordinary common decency," the Archbishop said to Father Campbell when they were alone. "Now let's change the subject. The reason I've sent for you is that I want you to come as my chaplain on this pilgrimage the Vicar-General seems to have been telling you about."

Could this offer be something more than merely coincidental, Father Campbell wondered. If Captain

Inches could be persuaded to go to Lourdes there was at least a chance that he would regain his faith. And if, which was unlikely but not impossible, he were to be given back his sight, it wouldn't be only the parish of East Hadwick that would be stirred. So far Scotland had never had a miracle at Lourdes. Almost able to visualise the Moderator of the General Assembly calling lum hat in hand at the cathedral clergy house, Father Campbell told the Archbishop his thought.

"By all means bring him along," the Archbishop said. "But don't get ideas into your head about converting the stiff-necked. Things have changed since Our Lord's day. Even if they see signs and wonders people still won't believe. They're so convinced that miracles are *a priori* impossible that if John Knox himself were to rise from the dead before their eyes they'd argue he was Harry Lauder doing a turn."

But when Captain Inches agreed to sink his pride and make the pilgrimage to Lourdes at the expense of the Vicar-General's Lucky Dip, Father Campbell began to think that Divine Providence lay behind it all; and when Captain Inches joined in the "*Ave, Ave, Ave*" on the station platform he was certain.

3

The Abbé Bonpapa came to meet them in Paris at the Gare du Nord, and took the Archbishop and Father Campbell to dine at *Chez Théophraste* while

their train was being shunted round the *ceinture* to
the Gare de Lyon. Dinner with soup, eggs, or fish
or meat, dessert and wine now cost eighteen francs;
with soup, eggs or fish, meat, dessert and wine twenty-
two francs; with soup, eggs, fish, meat, dessert and
wine twenty-five francs. The Abbé suggested that
this time, in view of the Archbishop's dignity, they
should choose the second alternative without any
sharing of dishes between them; and, when they had
each opted for eggs or fish, began to tell them about
the Church in France.

Armand Lucot, the Abbé said, "*vivait maritalement
avec une femme avec laquelle il n'était pas marié*, had
presided at that year's Left Bank Good Friday Sausage
Luncheon and was likely to become Minister of
Education in the next French Cabinet but one, and
from such a position would be able to attack the
Church where she felt it most, in the schools.

"But surely, Monsieur l'Abbé," the Archbishop
said, "the Church will be able to attack back."

"The Church in France, Monseigneur, has become
the vassal of the *bourgeoisie*," the Abbé said and went
on to quote Léon Bloy: "'Dear Lord, I'm a very
bad priest, I'm afraid. The flock you made me
shepherd of is so sound asleep that I can't wake it
up. And how ugly they look with their screwed up
eyes and they snore abominably too. Merely watching
their yawns has sent me off as well. I'm dozing when
I preach to them or pray for them, I nod at death-

beds and have forty winks leaning against coffins. Even when I consecrate the Bread and Wine at the Fearful Sacrifice I'm only half awake. I drop off at baptisms and in the confessional, and often I'm not quite sure whether I'm giving people Extreme Unction or marrying them. Yes, even when I'm joining for all eternity two of Your creatures with Your Image half-sliding off their faces, my eyes are so heavy when I bless them that it's all I can do not to get down to a bit of kip on the altar steps.' "

The Archbishop looked appalled.

" If any priest of mine behaved like that I'd have him sent to a monastery until he came to his senses," he said.

" Our Bishops send us to monasteries when we come to ours," the Abbé said. " Of course I won't go so far as to say that they encourage us to be lazy. But most of them are being too careful not to offend the civil power to remember that we've been sent to call, not the righteous, but sinners to repentance. The way they smirk when they have a chance of leading a Grand Orient mayor to a *prie-Dieu* in the sanctuary on St. Joan of Arc's day! And their eager waddle to marry a Senator's daughter! And not a man jack among them, Monseigneur, with the guts to clamp down on simony."

" Simony's a strong word, Monsieur l'Abbé," the Archbishop said.

" What else, Monseigneur, can you call their

graded stole fees? Never go to church after your first communion, send for your mistress on your death-bed instead of for the priest, but if you can stump up five thousand francs you'll have the whole clergy of the parish doing a solemn blubber round your coffin, a crowd of ham-faced unbelievers screeching the *Dies Irae* in the organ loft, and the absolution in a cope. Go to Holy Communion every day of your life, die as the Curé d'Ars died, but if you've only got a thousand francs there'll be no blubbers, no ham-faced unbelievers, no cope. Five hundred and the priest won't even go with the hearse to the cemetery. Nothing and you'll get a scratch of a prayer under the church porch. Marriage the same: five thousand for the high altar, thirteen hundred for the Lady altar, eleven hundred for the Sacred Heart and fifty for St. John Bosco and a belch in the sacristy. The excuse of course is the old hag in the mink coat who arrives at the Madeleine in her Rolls-Royce and puts five centimes in the collection plate. But whether the old hag in the mink coat produced the huckstering or the huckstering the old hag in the mink coat, even the Vicar Capitular can't say. Anyway, Christ never drew up a tariff for His blessings and the Bishops are making a big mistake if they imagine that even the stupidest of the laity think that he did."

" Does the Pope know about this? " the Archbishop asked.

" Probably not. No doubt our Lords the Cardinals,

Archbishops and Bishops of France have other matters
to bring to his notice when they make their visits
ad limina. And don't forget that His Holiness has the
Italian clergy on his hands as well. Not to mention
the Spanish. But in Spain most of those who are
rooked for their obsequies have at least died shriven,
communicated and anointed. Here ninety per cent
of those buried with the full flummery have not
received the Last Sacraments; and most of the ten
per cent that have have sent for the priest with the
doubtful confidence of a drunkard ordering a prairie
oyster the morning after the night before."

"But what about when they were young?" the
Archbishop asked. "Weren't they taught their
religion then?"

"For the vast majority, Monseigneur, their first
communion was also their last. I doubt if ten per cent
of the whole country could recite the three motives
for repentance in their ascending order of merit:
fear of hell, complicity in the Crucifixion, love of
God. People no longer need to know them: they
can have the whole works without that. All that's
necessary is for their relatives to pay the undertaker
and the undertaker to pay the priest and Judas kisses
Christ in Gethsemane all over again. It's as easy as
taking out a ticket at the pari-mutuel, and it's a
wonderful way of building new churches in the
suburbs for more unbelievers to be buried from."

The Abbé stopped to allow them all to finish their

meat, but when the fruit salad came he started in again:

" With only fools and frauds to oppose them the secularists are having things their own way, in spite of the fact that they are almost as unoriginal as we are. French novelists are still saying the same thing as Zola, that under the appearance of virtue there is always the reality of vice. The possibility of virtue existing under the look of vice never seems to strike any of them. ' Noble sentiments make bad literature,' that cretinous old bore Gide said. But surely the stockbroker who is a daily communicant is as legitimate a subject of art as the duchess who invites the *wagon-lit* attendant into her sleeping compartment on the *train bleu*. La Rochefoucauld could no longer define hypocrisy as the tribute which vice pays to virtue: on the contrary hypocrisy has now become the tribute which virtue pays to vice, because the only way the good man can be popular today is by appearing to share the weaknesses of his fellows."

Father Campbell had been trying to think up something intelligent to say, and he shot in eagerly:

" It's the same with us, Monsieur l'Abbé. John Galsworthy, Arnold Bennett, H. G. Wells, all of them have simplified unpardonably the theology they've never read." The phrase was taken from a letter he hadn't quite dared to send to the *Catholic Trumpet* after reading an article praising the novels of Isabel C. Clarke. " And, as for the Americans, well you've only got to read Sinclair Lewis's *Elmer Gantry*."

"And the so-called neo-impressionists who paint a sardine sitting at a typewriter and call it a young woman's legs getting into a taxi," the Abbé spluttered ferociously.

"The other way round would be more dangerous, wouldn't it?" the Archbishop said.

"But don't you see, Monseigneur? This isn't just an attack on *moral* theology; it's an attack on theology *tout court*. All this abstraction is nothing more or less than propaganda for nihilism. It's an attempt to make the world seem meaningless."

"I agree, Monsieur l'Abbé," Father Campbell said and quoted a verse from a poem he had read in the previous week's issue of *The Wednesday Beam:*

> "Her new black hat
> Looked like an umbrella held
> In the imperativeless Nietzschean night."

"The key word is 'imperativeless' of course," the Abbé said. "The devil doesn't want us to believe in moral compulsions because that's only a step from belief in God."

"Who, according to D. H. Lawrence, 'is a vast shimmering impulse which waves outwards towards some end,'" Father Campbell said and hoped that the Archbishop wouldn't think he was showing off.

"A Radical Socialist opening a new swimming

pool at a Lycée couldn't have done better," the Abbé said.

4

" If you ask me your friend's a bit of a blether," the Archbishop said as they stood together in the corridor of the train watching the black trees being rushed past the window. " And as for quotations there's one from a man called Keating he might do well to remember: ' If a priest has only time to shave or make a meditation, let him shave.' Less St. John of the Cross and more Gillette mightn't do Monsieur l'Abbé Bonpapa any harm."

But the Archbishop, Father Campbell could see, was worried; and when he had anticipated Matins and Lauds for the next day, he began to wonder if " the roseate hues of early dawn " had done so much harm after all, and whether the erring Church of England might not have contributed less to the present distress than the temporising True Church in France.

5

" Fortunately Bernadette was spared the sight of these spiritual groceries," the Archbishop said to Father Campbell as they walked past shops festooned with rosaries as large as tyres. "The only thing she wasn't let off was a photograph of the statue at the grotto. 'My lady wasn't like that at all,' she said when she saw it. 'My lady wasn't always praying.' A quotation which might with profit be engraved on the walls of every Church in Christendom. Whatever the next world may or may not be, it is highly unlikely that the Mother of God will turn out to look like Lilian Gish in *Orphans of the Storm*."

Father Campbell tried to look both grave and amused, as he guessed the Archbishop wanted him to.

"Of course sloppy expressions of piety will always be with us, and for charity's sake we must bear with them as we put up with town councillors' wives' hats," the Archbishop went on. "Huysmans was both right and wrong when he condemned the *bondieuseries* of the Place St. Sulpice: right because they are an insult to the majesty of God and cloud it from the eyes of the intelligent; wrong because seasick madonnas and mutton chop Sacred Hearts seem to be the only way of getting Irishmen and Italians to glimpse the intangible glory. As T. S. Eliot said : ' . . . the True Church remains below, wrapt in the old miasmal mist.' But King Edward saw it, even here: 'Down on your knees, Tom; this is the true religion,' he's supposed to have said to the old $1/11\frac{1}{2}$d the pound."

The Archbishop's words helped Father Campbell to be inspired rather than repelled by the sugary

statue in the grotto: the ungrammatical "JE SUIS
L'IMMACULÉE CONCEPTION" seemed to prove the
authenticity of Bernadette's vision as surely as the
abandoned crutches hung up round the altar. "Why
not an artificial leg?" Zola had asked. Why not
indeed, Father Campbell wondered too: new flesh
grafted instantaneously to a stump would have
silenced the sceptics for ever. Then he remembered
what Cardinal Bourne had said to the Old Jock:
for faith to have merit a margin must be left for trust
to fight doubt. One couldn't save up for heaven like
for a holiday at Aberdour. A miracle after all
was only a break in a sequence itself more miraculous.

"Not *The Living Desert*, but *The Deserted Village*.
However we got in."

"Anyway old George came back at three and
brought the bottles."

Father Campbell turned angrily and glared the
empty Anglo-Saxon pagan faces into silence. Surely
God, if He was all-powerful and not just all-ruling,
ought to strike those insolent infidels down dead as
an incontestable proof of His might. Father Campbell
realised that he was no better than Zola: the worldly,
the stupid and the frivolous, like the stumps of the
amputated, had to be borne with until the Lord
should come again to clear up the mess. Christ's rebuke to St. Thomas had gone ringing down the
centuries: "*Beati qui non viderunt, et crediderunt.*"

But that did not prevent Father Campbell from

praying that Captain Inches might be cured of his blindness, in order that others might see and believe.

For Captain Inches himself was believing again already. The sneering and the bitterness were gone; and, as physical cures were so often reserved for the malignant and the incredulous, Father Campbell was beginning to be afraid that he was going to be let down with a spiritual one. An amputated H. G. Wells stood much more chance of having a new arm stuck on at Lourdes than an amputated Cardinal Archbishop of Westminster.

At three o'clock Captain Inches went with the other walking sick and knelt behind the invalids laid out on stretchers on either side of the square. The Host was brought down to the altar and placed in the monstrance for the Archbishop to carry, with Father Campbell as his deacon, and a big unhappy-looking German priest as his sub-deacon. As they entered the square in their white vestments the roar of the *Tantum Ergo* made even the rubber-neckers with their cameras look as though they understood holy thoughts:

> " *Praestet fides supplementum*
> *Sensuum defectui.*"

Had Adam's disobedience deserved all this, Father Campbell wondered, as the Archbishop stopped to raise the monstrance over blankets hiding cancers and running sores. Were these giants' heads on dwarfs' bodies really necessary? His uncomprehending

88

prayer held all the lupuses lined up in front of the
unsorrowing girls in their summer frocks, and cripples
in the back streets of slums he could not see. These
sufferings he could understand at a pinch, because
they could be united by an act of the will with
Christ's, to blot out the grins of the crooners. But
to the agony of rabbits caught in gin traps transmigration of souls seemed the only answer. Had
something got left out of the gospels, and did the
cruel come back to work out their purgatory in barns
and rivers and on tree tops? As he held back the edge
of the Archbishop's cope, Father Campbell tried not
to take too much pleasure in the thought of a wriggling
Monsignor Samson-Slingsby being jabbed on the
edge of a hook so that a vivisector might be drawn
out of the Tay by his tongue and fried for the
breakfast of a pig once stuck in Baluchistan and now
being compensated as a retired Indian Army colonel
in Broughty Ferry.

"Do you mean to say you don't know how
potassium was found in Saskatchewan?"

"We've got an eight-ton crushing plant with a
triple adjustment and what's more we evaporate all
chemicals."

Father Campbell scowled at the crew cuts with all
the hatred he could get the devil to pour into him.
Then the chink of the censer drew him forward
with the Archbishop and the German to Captain
Inches. "Oh God," he prayed, as the Archbishop

raised the monstrance, "crash through just this once."

But even when he heard the cry of triumph behind them, Father Campbell had still to move on with the Archbishop, in case God might lean out of his gesture twice in the same afternoon.

6

At one moment, Captain Inches told them afterwards, he had seen darkness and the next light. Although he had not been able to pick out Father Campbell's features distinctly he had recognised him. He was seeing neither worse nor better when he was examined by the official doctors, who were unwilling to pronounce this recovery of blurred sight a miracle. Excitement and emotion, they said, might have momentarily reactivated Captain Inches's still seriously damaged optic nerves, and in that case total blindness might very well recur. Only in the event of his eyesight improving until it finally became normal ought canonical recognition of a miracle to be asked for. The Bishop of Tarbes impressed upon the Archbishop the advisability of accepting this advice.

7

The only person who wasn't disappointed was Captain Inches.

" I don't think it matters one way or the other," he said to Father Campbell in the train on the way home. " The main thing is that at the same time as my sight came back I was made to understand that what you told me that day at Béthune about contemplatives was true."

Father Campbell did his best to conceal his impatience. It wasn't just a conversion that was required if the barmaids of East Hadwick were to be turned into Saint Thérèses of Lisieux. There was nothing the barmaids didn't know about conversions and the brake they put on backchat with customers. What was wanted was a real drawing aside of the curtain like that which had happened to Jack Weston in Robert Hugh Benson's *A Winnowing*.

It didn't make things any better when the Scottish Episcopal ophthalmologist, who examined Captain Inches's eyes on his return, confirmed the findings of the doctors in Lourdes.

" While I admit there is something in this improvement in Captain Inches's sight which medical science can't explain," he told Father Campbell, " I should strongly advise you to be most careful before you risk explaining in terms of the supernatural an amelioration which may only be temporary. Anyway

I'm a staunch Protestant and I don't believe in miracles."

The local representative of the *Scottish Catholic Trumpet*, who had the sweaty underpaid look common to those who work for the Faith or tourist agencies, was round as soon as Captain Inches was seen out walking without his white stick.

" What's this I hear about a miracle happening at the pilgrimage ? " he asked.

Father Campbell was guarded:

" You can have heard nothing about a miracle happening at the pilgrimage because as yet we ourselves don't know that one has occurred."

" Come off it now. If you haven't heard that Captain Inches has been seen reading the *Catholic Trumpet*, I have."

" He'd be much better to be seen reading Karl Marx. It'd do his reputation less harm—not to mention his religion."

" Now, now, Father, I'm sure we do our best. But if that's the way you want it you can have it. We'll go on keeping our mouths shut until you give us the word."

But the *Catholic Trumpet*'s discretion could not prevent Captain Inches's daily improving eyesight from becoming the subject of common gossip, and one Friday afternoon Father Campbell returned from a death-bed to find a reporter from the *Glenlady and East Hadwick Beacon* waiting in his study.

" What's this I hear about a faith cure in your parish, Father ? "

" You have heard nothing about a faith cure in my parish," Father Campbell said. " A faith cure is a cure effected by the confidence of the patient in his own recovery. The cures that take place at Lourdes aren't that at all. They take place quite independently of the dispositions or belief of the invalid. They are for the most part instantaneous healings of damaged tissues."

" Just a minute while I get that down," the reporter said.

" Don't mix it up with what the Captain of the Rangers told you about the Captain of the Hibs, will you ? "

" You will have your little joke, won't you, Father ? Now about the miracle."

" It's not a miracle, I tell you."

" But I thought you'd just told me that it wasn't a faith cure."

" All I said was that the cures that take place at Lourdes aren't faith cures. I spoke of no particular case."

" But everybody says that this Captain Inches is seeing better every day and that he's not only walking about without his white stick but reading newspapers as well."

" I know. But whatever you may have heard to the contrary the Church is exceedingly cautious about these matters. Before we claim that Captain Inches's recovery of his sight has been caused by the direct intervention of God we must be sure that he is out of all danger of relapse. There's always the possibility that his optic nerves may only have been temporarily reactivated by emotion."

" In other words it may be a faith cure after all."

" It cannot be a faith cure. The improvement in Captain Inches's eyesight took place instantaneously, at the exact moment when the Archbishop raised the Host over him in blessing. If Captain Inches recovers his sight the recovery is a miracle and the Universal Church will not hesitate to proclaim it as such."

" But Captain Inches *has* recovered his sight."

" Not permanently, he hasn't. At least we're not in a position to say so yet."

" And when do you think you will be in a position to say so ? "

" Perhaps in three months' time. Not before."

" And then it *will* be a miracle ? "

" If the present improvement is maintained, I suppose so, yes."

On Wednesday morning the *Glenlady and East Hadwick Beacon* came out with the headline:

PRIEST SAYS PARISHIONER

WILL BE CURED BY

A MIRACLE

IN THREE MONTHS' TIME;

and on Wednesday evening Captain Inches called at the presbytery to tell Father Campbell that he was as blind as before.

8

"I don't want to rub things in, Father," Monsignor Samson-Slingsby said as he led Father Campbell along the corridor to the Archbishop's study, "but outside the Deposit of the Faith I have always been in favour of maintaining the scepticism of the positivist."

Father Campbell was too busy with his own misery even to attempt to reply. Had Newman been only a cruel joke after all? Were the permutations of infelicity as haphazard as Al Capone and putting? Then why, oh, why was Captain Inches still so sure that God was behind the inconsequences?

To Father Campbell's surprise the Archbishop's old walnut face was wrinkled with benevolence.

"This has just come in from the Holy See," the Archbishop said and handed Father Campbell a document which read:

"By virtue of the authority transmitted to us in unbroken descent from Peter the First Apostle, we make known to Your Grace that, with a view to aiding Your Grace in the administration of the Archdiocese of Inchkeith and the Pentlands, the Reverend Donald Dunwhinnie Campbell be consecrated Bishop of Missolongi in the region of the unfaithful. . . ."

"It'll be a good way of silencing criticism," the Archbishop said as he took the parchment back again. "Let's say Monday at ten o'clock, shall we? That will give me time to get hold of the co-consecrators."

Italians would have embraced, Frenchmen at least shaken hands. Scotsmen found either gesture theatrical. The Archbishop and Father Campbell could only try not to smile at each other with too obvious affection.

CHAPTER VI

ON THE Feast of St. Rose of Lima, with Commemoration of Sts. Felix and Adauctus, Martyrs, Donald Dunwhinnie Campbell was skirled into the pro-cathedral of St. Bean by four Campbell pipers. Kneeling before the Archbishop he took an oath to maintain the honours, privileges and authority of the Holy Roman Church; to suppress heretics, schismatics and rebels against the Lord; to attend Synods; God and God's Holy Gospels helping him, not to sell, give away, pawn or part with his household furniture without the permission of the Supreme Pontiff; to teach the people the Scriptures by word and by example; to receive with reverence, promulgate and preserve the constitutions of the Apostolic See; to be loyal, submissive and obedient to God's Vicar Pius and to his successors; to practise and to teach chastity and sobriety; to promote God's business and neglect the world's; to be humble and patient; to be affable and considerate to the poor, to travellers and to the needy; that he believed in the Trinity, the One Catholic and Apostolic Church and the Resurrection of the Body. Then the Archbishop and their Lordships of Hawick and Tobermory laid their hands upon him, and gave him the Holy Ghost and the power to bestow it. Then the Archbishop anointed his head and his hands, that he might be able to curse, to bless and to bind, to hate pride and to shun praise, and that the fragrance of his life might be as the dew of Hermon.

2

" Man, I do declare these white shoes of yours make you look more hentoed than ever," the Archbishop said to the new Bishop in the sacristy afterwards. " Anyway don't let them go to your head. ' A shabby cassock goes well with a beautiful chasuble,' the Curé of Ars used to say. Never wear your vestments; let them wear you."

" My dear fellow, the mediocrity of Bishops is only a matter of ecclesiastical discipline. You see, any fool can dole out the Holy Ghost." It was Monsignor Samson-Slingsby of course, talking to the Episcopal Dean, the Very Reverend Arthur Pearson, who had come to offer his congratulations. The mockery on the Vicar-General's stockbrokerish face when he knelt for the new Bishop's blessing was in contrast with the humility of Fathers O'Callaghan, Weir and Scully whose hands had been laid on the Bishop's head when he had been ordained. As he made the sign of the cross over their rough common hair the new Bishop hoped that he might be worthy of their trust; enough grubby paws had been laid on the Church already.

"Come on, boys, it's gin o'clock." On the grounds that their patronage of so worldly an establishment as the Thistle Hotel might be misinterpreted by those not of the Household of the Faith, the Vicar-General had arranged for the official luncheon to be held at the Ossian. "I and the rest of the rank and file will go on ahead by foot. Like that we'll leave the Morris free for the Bench."

The Union Bank of Scotland account had now run to a second-hand car, which the Archbishop drove as an illiterate spoke his mother tongue, sliding over pistons and sparking plugs as though they were infinitives and gerunds.

"I was consecrated by Jimmy Buchanan and Jimmy Buchanan was consecrated by Willie Ballantyne and Willie Ballantyne was consecrated by John Duncan and like that you go right back to Cardinal Beaton," the Archbishop said as he swerved to avoid a young woman crossing the road with her nose stuck into *Sorrell and Son*.

" Surely the main thing is that he can trace his descent back to the Apostles," said the Bishop of Hawick who was fond of moralising. " Always be guided by the Holy Ghost, young man."

" It's not such a bad idea," the Archbishop said. " What with Joan of Arc and Galileo and one thing and another we seem to need a little bit of prompting now and again."

But His Lordship of Hawick wasn't going to be done out of his unction:

" And don't forget that only a heart's beat separates even a Bishop from the Judgment seat," he said.

" Aye, that's a fact," the Bishop of Tobermory said.

The Lord Provost of the City had a slightly different point of view and he stalked through the steamer funnel trousers crowding the Prince Charlie room of the Ossian to deliver it:

" What I like about you fellows who kick with the left foot is your broadmindedness. Now why don't you and everybody else get together and revise all those out-of-date doctrines in the light of modern science? Companionate marriage now. Why shouldn't young couples have a trial trip in the Trossachs? After all a chap doesn't buy a motor car without seeing how it'll do on the hills? And you can't turn a wife in every year and get a new model from Olympia."

A Thread of Scarlet

To this there seemed to be no easy answer, and
for once Bishop Campbell was grateful to the Vicar-
General for butting in:

"Tell me, my Lord Provost, and what is your
opinion of Mex. Eagles as a buy?"

But even Monsignor Samson-Slingsby couldn't
save him from two people at once.

"Now, Bishop, tell me honestly," the Episcopal
Dean said. "When the holy hands were laid upon
you did you feel infallibility bubbling up inside you
like lemonade? Because if you did it's a sure sign
you're going to be Pope."

After that the two young curates arguing at the
top of their voices behind him were a relief:

"Now look here, Father Brodie, the Catholic
Bishops have distinctly said . . ."

"To hell with what the Catholic Bishops have
distinctly said. The Catholic Bishops have been
consistently wrong since Manning and Vaughan.
Why the hell should they suddenly start being right
now?"

A good shaking up was what the Church required
most, the new Bishop thought, and it was better
that it should come from below than from nowhere
at all.

"Your very good health, Fathers," he said as he
turned and raised his glass.

At the luncheon itself the presence of the Lord
Provost put a brake on shop, but when Bishop

Campbell had replied to the toast " *Ad multos annos* "
the Vicar-General started in on him:

" Surely, My Lord, the chief problem the Church's
leaders have to face today is how to answer intelligent
scepticism: before we can produce metaphysical
proof that personality survives the death of the body,
we have got to define personality. ' *Rationalis naturae
individua substantia*,' Boethius defined it as, as Your
Lordship will of course remember."

The new Bishop couldn't even remember if he had
remembered Boethius.

" What it all boils down to is this," Monsignor
Samson-Slingsby went on. " Is the soul still a person
when the body has died? It is still of course ' an
individual substance of a rational nature.' But can
we say that it is a *complete* individual substance of a
rational nature? In all honesty I don't think that we
can, not at least until the body has been resurrected
and joined to it again. The body, after all, as the
house in which the soul is lodged, is an essential part
of its rational nature as we know it."

Their Lordships of Hawick and Tobermory, Bishop
Campbell was glad to see, were looking almost as
perplexed as the Lord Provost.

" Descartes thought differently, as I suppose you
know, My Lord," the Vicar-General jabbed in again
at the new Bishop.

" Descartes, of course," Bishop Campbell said with
an unhappy glance of appeal at the Archbishop.

"Why 'of course,' My Lord?" Monsignor Samson-Slingsby asked. "Descartes was a heretic, and heretics are never 'of course.' Heretics are only 'alas.' St. Thomas of Aquin was the chap who hit the nail on the head. And how many nails he did hit on the head: the Averroist Aristotelian kefuchle, '*damnum emergens*' and '*lucrum cessans*,' the rubrics of the nuptial couch . . ."

The Lord Provost brightened.

"Tell me, Monsignor," he asked. "What do you think of Marie Stopes?"

The Vicar-General turned to the Archbishop. "That reminds me, Your Grace. I should be grateful for Your Grace's permission to read *Radiant Motherhood*."

"Why, Monsignor? Are you thinking of becoming a radiant mother?"

While they were all laughing at the Vicar-General's embarrassment a flat-footed waitress came up behind the new Bishop and put her mouth close to his ear.

"You'll have to be a good Kartholic now, Father, My Lord, I mean," she whispered.

3

"Between you and me I'd give Rome time to forget this wild oat of yours," the Archbishop said to Bishop Campbell that evening. "So if you don't mind I'll drop a word to my old friend Monsignor

Pantachini and tell him that until further notice I'll
be looking after the visits *ad limina* myself. ' Miss
Assisi,' I believe they call him now, because of his
good looks. Now, now, don't get ideas into your
head. ' *Manus nemo cito imposueris*,' the Apostle said.
If you're not regretting my choice I'm not."

CHAPTER VII

BISHOP CAMPBELL took the Archbishop's advice and
let sleeping dogs lie. Then in January 1934 Captain
Inches was run over while crossing the street and
killed and the story of the false miracle revived in
the Press. His memory apparently jogged, Monsignor
Pantachini wrote to the Archbishop and said that, if
it was all the same to His Grace of Inchkeith and the
Pentlands, the Holy See would very much like to
have a look at his auxiliary.

Setting out from Scots College for his audience,
Bishop Campbell was shocked by the indifference
with which passers-by in the via Quattro Fontane
regarded his purple sash and pectoral cross. Were
the very foundations of the Form beginning to
moulder ? Perhaps lions in the Colosseum again might
not be such a bad thing. Persecution generally paid.
Who knew what might not happen to the Church
of England if an Archbishop of Canterbury were

served up every year at the Lord Mayor's Banquet.

Were essentials being smothered under inessentials, he wondered as he showed his card to the striped Swiss Guard in the Cortile di San Damaso. Was the pike a suitable emblem of the love which would lay down its life for its friend? Did all these pictures and frescoes clarify or obscure the Meaning?

" Monsignor Pantachini would like to have a word with Your Excellency before Your Excellency sees His Holiness," a Privy Chamberlain of the Cape and Sword said to Bishop Campbell as he got out of the wheezy lift.

The Monsignor, as handsome as the Archbishop had predicted, had already two other Bishops with him: one tall and thin, the other short and fat, and their chins so blue with bristle that Bishop Campbell was reminded of Wearie Willie and Tired Tim of *Chips*; both, he thought, must be very good at meditation.

Monsignor Pantachini kissed Bishop Campbell's ring but did not genuflect.

" His Holiness will receive you presently," he said. " In the meantime may I introduce you to Their Lordships the Bishops of Bovisa and Spartivento. My Lords, this is His Lordship the Bishop of Missolongi, auxiliary to His Grace the Archibishop of Inchkeith and the Pentlands."

" *Quid putas de Cardinal Schuster?* " Tired Tim asked.

"*Est severus et sanctus,*" Bishop Campbell managed to answer.

"*Est nimis severus et nimis sanctus,*" Wearie Willie said.

"Neither of Your Lordships need speak Latin," Monsignor Pantachini said. "His Lordship the Bishop of Missolongi was educated at the Scots College here and understand Italian perfectly."

"*Dunque il Signor è amore,*" Tired Tim said. "*Ecco la prova della nostra santa religione.*"

"God must be love all right to put up with some of the things His Church gives Him as Bishops," Monsignor Pantachini said when the two prelates had left for their audience. "And now, My Lord, what's all this we've been hearing about your having proclaimed as a true miracle of healing what was in fact only a temporary nervous amelioration of optic nerves?"

"That's an old story," Bishop Campbell nearly answered, but remembered in time that no stories could ever be old for a Church which filed and docketed eternity.

"My conscience on the matter is quite clear," he said instead, and told Monsignor Pantachini what had happened. "The press was indiscreet, that's all."

"By which, My Lord, I presume I am meant to take it that you were not."

It was the old story of the Major thinking that because he was military assistant to a General he himself was entitled to be insolent with Lieutenant-Colonels, the Bishop realised.

" Are you sure that discretion is all that's required of us, Monsignor? " he asked. " It's not by weighing every single word we utter that we're going to convert the one thousand million pagans still left in the world."

" One thousand and forty-eight million to be exact: three hundred and ninety-three million Confucians, two hundred and ninety-seven million Mohammedans, two hundred and fifty million Hindus, one hundred and eight million Buddhists."

" I see you've got it off pat, Monsignor. And a hundred years ago? How many pagans were there then? "

" Eight hundred and forty-three million." But for the lack of a moustache, the Monsignor's face might have been John Gilbert's elegant mug recalling a bridge score. " Three hundred and forty-seven million Confucians, two hundred and thirty-six million Mohammedans, one hundred and ninety-three million Hindus, sixty-seven million Buddhists."

But the Bishop was still more angry than impressed.

" In other words things have gone from bad to worse. Not a very good advertisement for *Propaganda Fide*, Monsignor."

" My Lord Bishop of Missolongi obviously knows little of the science of statistics otherwise he would not make the elementary mistake of comparing dissimilars. The factor Your Lordship has omitted to take into consideration is the increase in world population. If the heathen have increased so have the faithful. A hundred years ago there were only two hundred and fifty-million Catholic Christians in the world; today there are four hundred million."

"You too, Monsignor, would appear to be interpreting statistics incorrectly." In for a penny, in for a pound, the Bishop thought, determined not to be overawed by his surroundings. After all he was a shepherd of Christ's flock, and at his consecration he had sworn to speak the truth fearlessly. "How many of those four hundred million Catholic Christians you brag about care a fig about their salvation? How many of them even try to understand the Church's teaching? How many of them know whether Arius was condemned or approved by the Council of Nice for teaching that Our Lord was made and not begotten of the Father and that He was inferior to the Father and not equal to Him?"

The Monsignor's smile was not entirely acid.

"Surely my Lord Bishop of Missolongi is theologian enough to know that explicit familiarity with the permutations of heresy is not necessary to salvation."

"All right then. Let me put it this way. How many of your four hundred million faithful would know that it was untrue if the Church were to announce tomorrow that pigs' bodies would rise again with their own on the Last Day?"

"None, I hope. Because if the Church were to announce the resurrection of porkers then porkers would resurrect. But perhaps my Lord Bishop of Missolongi has chosen another bad illustration. At least I hope so. His Holiness, I am sure, would be most grieved to learn that a bishop had such an imperfect understanding of the power of the Holy Ghost to prevent the Church from teaching error." For a moment the Monsignor's expression was so cold and blank that Bishop Campbell thought he was serious, the next his smile was so nearly a grin that Bishop Campbell was sure that he must often have been called " Miss Assisi " to his face.

" We're wandering from the point a little, aren't we?" the Bishop said. " The point was my wrongly announced miracle and whether I was indiscreet. I don't think that I was. Anyway indiscretion's better than laziness."

" Circumspection, My Lord, shall we call it?"

" Laziness, Monsignor. That's what's losing the battle for us today. And the biggest dozers of the lot are to be found here in Rome. Do you know what a sacristan said to me the other day because I spent the regulation thirty minutes at the altar. He accused me of *praying* during my Mass."

" Perhaps the sacristan may not have been so irreligious as His Lordship thinks." The smile was measured again and the slippery eyes unreadable. "Often even the holiest of priests find it difficult to concentrate on the supernatural for more than a short period of time. The only way they can achieve a relative piety is by tearing through their devotions so quickly that their thoughts are just simply bounced from one word to another."

"Do you honestly believe that such was the understanding which inspired this sacristan's reproach to me?"

"Not for one moment. But charity ought to make my Lord Bishop willing to think that it was."

One up to Miss Assisi, the Bishop decided.

"Your Excellency spoke of laziness just now," Monsignor Pantachini went on. "'My kingdom is not of this world,' Our Lord said. And is His Excellency not leaving out the devil? Sometimes Satan can even use a crozier to stir champagne."

"Not in Scotland, Monsignor. He doesn't need to. He's got the Catholic Press instead. 'Rosary Routs Disbelief in Dumbarton.' Can't you see the atheists rushing into public houses for double whiskies when they read the newsbill!"

They were both laughing now.

2

"You'll find His Holiness rather depressed," Monsignor Pantachini said as he accompanied Bishop Campbell through a series of audience chambers each smaller than the preceding. "On Good Friday he said '*ne*' by mistake instead of '*ut*' in the prayer about snatching heretics and schismatics from their error, but I've told him not to worry too much, as it's the one prayer which God never seems to answer anyway."

But Monsignor Pantachini didn't smile as he said this, and Bishop Campbell didn't smile either when Monsignor Pantachini went in to the Holy Father's study alone and closed the door behind him.

3

At last the study door opened again and Monsignor Pantachini pushed Bishop Campbell in. The Bishop fell on his knees before the dumpy white figure which rose from his desk to bless and embrace him. There was nothing of the nullity of royalty in the strong square face of Achille Ratti, formerly Cardinal Archbishop of Milan, Nuncio to Warsaw, and Vatican Librarian, now Pope Pius XI. The eyes behind the thick spectacles held the persecuted Church in Russia, the wobbly Church in France, the cocky

Church in Ireland, the Church in Spain, China, Poland, Austria, Germany and Peru.

"The meanings of the matter is this, my son," the Pope said in English. "Beeshops must be doing all they can for the Church and then praying for it. But you are right to be worried. I should not have made you a Beeshop unless my think had been that you were a living wire, and living wires are always worried. I am a Beeshop myself and I am worried too. My son, all over the world there are wickednesses most terrible but the 'Olly Gost is an 'ope most wonderful. And my think is that perhaps all the Beeshops are not in 'ell and all the oars in 'eaven."

4

Walking back along the Corso Vittorio Emanuele with the box of cigars the Pope had given him under his arm, Bishop Campbell met a crocodile of German seminarians and smiled at their clean young faces. "*Et ego dico tibi, quia tu es Petrus, et super hanc petram aedificabo ecclesiam meam, et portæ inferi non praevalebunt contra eam.*" The Pope was right: the pun still held, and the Church had come on a lot since the Borgias went on the Stock Exchange.

CHAPTER VIII

IN THE early light of Sunday morning the skyscrapers looked like the steeples Cardinal Mercier had once mistaken them for. As he stood in the queue waiting to have his passport stamped, Bishop Campbell remembered having read that vertical lines had always sucked worldliness out of people, and wondered if Florrie Ford would have been such a success if she hadn't been fat.

"Now, Reverend, have you any intention of committing an immoral act while you are in this country?" the Immigration officer asked.

"That's a rather loose term you know," the Bishop said.

"Loose is the word, Reverend. There's bam in the sams, I know, but there's also a lot of out-of-town clergymen in the clip joints in 52nd Street. All right. We'll let that one go. Are you conspiring to overthrow the Government of the United States of America by force?"

"Do you think I'd tell you if I were?"

"All right. You're a British subject, I see. Why have you come here from Italy?"

"Because it was while I was there that I received instructions from my Archbishop to come here on a preaching tour to raise funds for his new cathedral sanctuary."

" Those cigars you've declared?" the Customs officer on Pier 90 asked. " Do you intend to smoke them yourself or are they a present for somebody else?"

" I intend to smoke them myself."

" In that case you'd better say they're a present for somebody else."

" But they're not, I tell you."

" And I tell you that you'd better say that they are a present for somebody else."

" How can I say they're for somebody else when they're for myself? You don't want me to tell a lie, do you?"

" Listen, Reverend. I'm telling you to say that they're a present for somebody else."

" And I'm telling you that I'm going to smoke them myself." It was already nine o'clock, and the Bishop was in a hurry to say Mass. " If you want to know the truth the Pope gave them to me and what's more they've been blessed by His Holiness for my personal use."

" For heaven's sake! And I took you for a Protestant!" The football face was smiling now, and soon there were scrawls all over the Bishop's luggage. " Say, what do you know? My Uncle's a Monsignor in the Archdiocese. Rooney's the name. 'Bye, Father. Have a big time."

2

MACKENZIE'S ARE READY TO FRY GOOD COD, the advertisement between the Greek Evangelical Church and the Church of the Open Door said. The notice board outside the Reorganised Church of Jesus Christ announced that the Reverend Doctor Ebenezer Soper would preach Identical Sermons at 11.30 a.m. and 7.30 p.m. Next to the Church of the Master EXOTIC LORELEI AND ONE HUNDRED NUDIE CUTIES were providing a SEXSATIONAL WEEK. "SCARED OF GUNS AND AFRAID OF GIRLS, WHAT SORT OF A SHERIFF WAS HE?" a movie theatre on Broadway asked.

"Eddie or Ernie his name was," the scoop of the taxi driver's lower lip spilled through the opening in the glass slide. "I said: 'Eddie or Ernie, you wait till I get money.' He said that he was going to Las Vegas and I said that the road was blocked and then he said 'I think that in the darkness they'll not see me, see?' Of course I was a child then, see? and my father and mother had nothin' from nothin' and so they had to sign that when I grew up I would be a Republican, see?"

After this the Bishop was not surprised to find that the window in his bedroom in the Acropolis and Parthenon Hotel was jammed so tight that he couldn't open it and that the basin was blocked and the bath plug missing from the end of its chain.

3

It was the ninth Sunday after Pentecost and the Bishop said his Mass in green vestments at a side altar in St. Patrick's. "*Domine Dominus noster, quam admirabilis est nomen tuum in universa terra,*" was the gradual. Cranmer's "O Lord our Governor, how excellent is Thy Name in all the world" had caught it too, the Bishop thought as he tried not to listen to the Monsignor shouting at the High Mass congregation from the pulpit: "Commencing next Sunday there will be a mission conducted for a week every evening at eight o'clock by the Redemptorist Fathers. In order to encourage everybody in the cathedral parish to attend we promise you that for the duration of the mission there will be no scolding in the confessional. But, mind you, we want no bad excuses: it's still a mortal sin to have missed Mass on Sunday even if the dentist hasn't sent your dentures back in time."

The Monsignor was still at it when the Bishop went to the back of the church to make his thanksgiving: "Even members of the Men's Sodality won't save their souls with fast women in slow trains." The faces turned to the pulpit were solemn and respectful. They seemed to be drinking it all in. Was the strength of the Church in the world the strength of the Church in America, and the strength of the Church in America the strength of the Church in Ireland and the priests with the faces like navvies and the mark coming up from their souls? After all the Church's job was to get the maximum to do the minimum for their salvation, and bullying might be as good a way as any other. The Bishop wondered what Pius XI's think would be.

Hell must look like Lexington Avenue, the Bishop thought as he walked back to his hotel. Perhaps neon lights would be beautiful in memory when they had been put out for a hundred years, but on the whole it seemed unlikely.

4

The Old Jock had impressed upon the Bishop that, not only were clergymen not expected to travel cheaply in America, but that the more they showed themselves among the wealthy the more likely were the layers-up of treasure on earth to switch their deposits to where neither rust and moth did corrupt and where thieves did not break through and steal.

"Now, Reverend, I don't want you to get me wrong," the man sitting next the Bishop said as the parlour car rolled past the unemptied garbage cans in 125th Street. "I mean I'm not religious. I mean I'm not an ant-eye religious, I mean I'm in between. Well, our pastor made us sing the creed last week, and no kidding. Mrs. Love that's my wife but everybody calls *me* Homer, well as I was saying neither Mrs.

Love nor me didn't know the goddam words but I guess all songs are the same once you get hold of the goddam idea if you see what I mean. Fee-fi-billy-aye-oh, singing on the old banjo."

Had the scowl and the threats of the Monsignor in St. Patrick's been wiser than he had imagined, the Bishop wondered. Different lands required different methods of evangelisation, the Pope had pointed out to the six Chinese Bishops when he had consecrated them. Was he the fool and the Monsignor the sage? But if bawls were all right for believers were they the proper medicine for tepid schismatics with yellow ties?

He was relieved when a man on the other side of the car came to his rescue.

" It burns me up to hear you talking like that," he said to the man with the yellow tie. " The Bible is the inspired Word of God, and I can prove it. Take the first verse of the first chapter of the Book of Genesis: ' In the beginning God created the heaven and the earth.' Ten words in English, but seven words in Hebrew. And what's more in those seven Hebrew words there are twenty-eight letters, which itself is a multiple of seven."

" So what? " the man with the yellow tie said. " I can give you figures too. Know how many guys there are in the world today? Two billion. Two thousand million. In other words there are now three times as many people living on this planet as there were two hundred years ago. And in another hundred years' time there'll be twice as many again. How are we going to keep 'em down on the farm or on the Bully Vards of Gay Paree? That's what I want to know."

The Bishop felt as unhappy as though the question had been put to himself. Was God's love nothing more than reliance on the law of averages? Omnipotence, he had once read, was as spendthrift as a General sending Divisions into battle: a few soldiers would survive to train other soldiers and that was all that mattered. How could one really feel that God cared, as the Church taught that He did care, uniquely about each one of two billion people, most of them ugly, cruel and mean? The haphazard way that He allowed them to die seemed to suggest that He didn't.

" Take the New Testament then if you don't believe me. The Septuagint, Matthew, verses one to eleven. In those eleven verses there are forty-nine Greek words which is seven times seven. In those forty-nine Greek words there are two hundred and sixty-six Greek letters which is thirty-eight times seven. In those two hundred and sixty-six Greek letters there are one hundred and forty vowels, which is twenty times seven, and one hundred and twenty-six consonants which is eighteen times seven."

" I can give you sevens too," the man with the yellow tie said. " In the United States of America alone seven thousand more people sit down to breakfast every day. What I want to know is where are the waffles coming from."

"Of those forty-nine Greek words thirty-five or five times seven occur more than once. Fourteen, or twice seven, occur only once."

"Emigrate, you will say. But where the hell's there left to emigrate to? In Europe the population's increasing at the rate of two million a year and in Asia at the rate of nine million a year."

"In those first eleven verses of Matthew in the Septuagint seven or a multiple of seven occurs fourteen times which is twice seven. According to the laws of permutation and combination for those fourteen sevens or multiples of seven to occur by accident there is only one chance in six hundred and seventy-eight billion, two hundred and twenty-three million, seventy-two thousand eight hundred and forty-nine."

"Increase the food production, you will say, but even doubling it won't do any good. And what about soil erosion, I'd like to know." The jutting chin was rampant with geology.

The Old Jock had been right, the Bishop realised: both men were looking at his dog collar for the solution which they themselves were unable to provide.

God was undeterminable, Gregory of Nyssa had said, and he who thought that he knew God deluded himself. But what was the use of his telling them that when he understood the statement so imperfectly himself?

" We've got to be able to give our reasons for not reasoning," the Old Jock had said to Cardinal Bourne in 1907.

But the best development of that that even Monsignor Samson-Slingsby had been able to think out was that as man's reason had been itself blunted by original sin, atheism arrived at either by deduction or induction was necessarily erroneous.

It didn't look as though it would be much good telling either of them the Vicar-General's conclusion that belief was an objective intuition which could be reasoned *about* but not reasoned *out*.

And a celibate always had a thin time of it when he tried to argue against birth control.

The Bishop tried not to be glad when the two men began to talk about something else.

" You should have heard George, that's my boss, telling this story about a guy staying to drink beer with another guy and of how it was getting dark and how they were all sitting round. Anyway I guess it's quite a story."

" It's always the same. Paying those goddam calls is like walking on flypaper. When you've made your sale you can't get on to the next bum because the first bum keeps on talking."

" *Ut quid diligitis vanitatem et quaeritis mendacium?* "

the Bishop read in his breviary, and when he went into the dining-car offered up the food as a penance for his inarticulateness.

5

Next Sunday, in the Cathedral of Cherubim and Seraphim, Minnehaha, Bishop Campbell preached at all Masses on the parable of the publican who went up into the temple to pray.

Although the publican had pleased God by asking God to be merciful to him, a sinner, that did not mean that the Pharisee was wrong in his observances, the Bishop said. Our Lord's comment had been measured: " *Dico vobis, descendit hic justificatus in domum suam ab illo . . .*" The publican went down to his house justified rather than the other. The Form was as necessary to hold the Spirit as was the Spirit to burnish the Form. The Form was the Church, and the Spirit was the Mind of the Church turned towards God and their neighbour. The Mind of the Church turned towards their neighbour expressed itself by charity; the Mind of the Church turned towards God expressed itself in obedience and worship. It was so that worship in the Archdiocese of Inchkeith and the Pentlands might be beautiful that he had come all the way from Scotland to appeal to their generosity.

In the palace after lunch the Bishop of Minnehaha

handed a cheque for $567.75 to his brother of Missolongi.

"And to think that I never got to first base with His Holiness!" the Right Reverend Dr. Finbar Magillycuddy-Tuohy said as he puffed away at one of the cigars the Pope had given Bishop Campbell. "I expect I kind of got in Dutch with him on my last visit *ad limina*, see? I told him that if he didn't know where the money for running the Vatican was coming from, I did."

"I shouldn't worry about that too much, if I were you," Bishop Campbell said. "From the little I know of His Holiness he'll have forgiven you long ago."

"Unfortunately it wasn't only His Holiness I shot my mouth off to. I blew my top to that Monsignor Pantachini or Miss Assisi or whatever he calls himself as well. I said that it was all screwball for dames having to wear black gloves up to the elbows and and then finding His Holiness sitting under a picture of an angel with his ass all let out."

"Perhaps he didn't understand. Perhaps Your Excellency's colloquialism was too difficult for him."

"Oh, he understood all right. There's nothing those jokers don't understand when they want to and nothing they do when they don't: for example, about the Church here not only having taught her children the Faith, but good manners and European culture as well." A cloud of smoke sailed over His

Excellency's face, softening its beefy apostolicity.
" And to think that I once said the guy's personality
hadn't enough zing. However I take it all back now.
Pius is sure a big time Pope."

" Big time enough certainly to realise that the hope
for the old Church in the East lies in the new Church
in the West."

" Oh, we're making the grade all right, Your
Excellency; but don't let's get too cocky about it.
As I said years ago to the Fruit Canners' Convention
in Atlantic City when I was spiritual adviser to them,
one day the devil's going to tempt our outfit, that's
for sure. And the clergy will be in the front line,
see? Women and drink are out. Materialism will be
the weapon. Nobody can tell a pastor when he's
building too big a rectory, see? Only Our Lord
can do that. Our Lord can do anything. Why, he
can even take a bunch of us phonies and turn us into
priests! When I was young I used to think the Church
was 80% Finbar and 20% God. Now I know that
it's 99% God and perhaps 1% the clergy throughout
the world."

" In that case, Your Excellency, why didn't the
99% prevent the Church from losing the Church in
Europe? " Bishop Campbell asked.

" Because the employers refused to listen to the 1%
interpreting the 99%. Leo XIII's *Rerum Novarum* was
the thing to get Christ off the hook. Leo believed that
Our Lord meant what He said when He promised

that He would always answer prayer. That's what's the matter with American Bishops today: they think the Church of God requires *running*. They're so tickled with the idea of themselves as administrators that they're perpetually trying to do the Holy Ghost's work for Him."

"I think I understand what Your Excellency means."

"I wonder if you do, because I'm not quite sure if I do myself." The American Bishop sat for a little in silence, stuck down into his cassock like a plant in a pot. "Naturally the Church will always have to deal mainly *with* fools, but that oughtn't to mean that the dealing should be done *by* fools. And that's what priests are who bring all their artillery to bear on the lusts of the flesh and let cruelty go unrebuked. Why, I'd rather have every enclosed nun in America singing *Roll 'Em Girlies, Roll 'Em* than have one puppy shaken awake by surgeons to see how long it can live without sleep."

"There, Your Excellency, I agree with you. You've no idea how much."

"Birth control too. The Church condemns birth control because it blocks God's method of launching souls on the runway towards the Beatific Vision. But we could afford to soft-pedal the subject until we've got the Sermon on the Mount across: after all here in America we've incentives to purity that don't exist in Europe. One look at a Women's Club and Casanova would have saved his soul."

"And the religious Press?" Bishop Campbell asked. "What's that like in America?"

"My sister's the person you want to talk to about that. She's the cutest nun. Her Order markets a cure for hangovers but they run a gas station as well although of course the Mother Superior sees to it there's no horsing around. Our Lady of Gold Rush Gulch, the joint's called. Why don't we run over there and make a date with a steak?"

6

NO SMOKING

NO VULGARITY

NO BLASPHEMY

NO GAS FOR FREE

ran the notice in the nuns' service station at which Sister Scholastica had just finished filling up a Ford.

"Would you believe it, Your Excellency," she said to Bishop Campbell when her brother had introduced him, "that dope had never heard of E. M. Foster."

"Folks all know for miles around, Watson's seeds are best in town," a loudspeaker above the door said. "Get Watson's chick starter from your dealer today and give your chicks a start in life."

125

" Now, Lou," the Bishop of Minnehaha said as they all walked into the office and sat down, "tell His Lordship the Bishop of Missolongi what you said to that bunch of Monsignors about Stendhal."

" It's smooth and it's creamy and it's double-flavoured," the loudspeaker said. " Doctors recommend it for Baby's first solid food."

" I told them what Stendhal had said himself in *Le Rouge et Le Noir*," Sister Scholastica said. " ' Well, sir, what else is a novel but a mirror being carried along a main road?' I said that the mirror had got to reflect the images that were thrown on it and not those that a lot of Jansenist knuckleheads wanted to see."

> " Honey, guess I'm in a stew
>   And wanna be blew,
>   Because of yew,"

the loudspeaker said.

" Newman hit the nail on the head when he said that you couldn't expect to have a sinless literature in a sinful world," Sister Scholastica said.

" If illness should come: just think what it means to receive a hundred dollars or an iron lung," the loudspeaker said.

" As Mauriac says, what matters is whether or not the artist connives at the evil he describes," Sister Scholastica said.

" Now right here in Sioux Falls it looks like rain," the loudspeaker said.

"How does that jack up with *Ulysses* now?" the Bishop of Minnehaha asked.

"Well, there's nothing as sweet as Baby's smile," the loudspeaker said.

"The trouble with Joyce is that he just sits around on his can and writes," Sister Scholastica said.

"Tell him, Lou, about what His late Eminence said to you when you sent him a copy of Babbitt."

"That baaastard!" Sister Scholastica said. "May his soul rest in peace and may perpetual light shine upon him!"

"Folks, this is Fifi Thompson saying ' Hello ' from Whispering Glades," the loudspeaker said.

7

Later, kneeling at the back of the dark chapel and listening to the snuffed out nuns singing the *Te Lucis Ante Terminum*, Bishop Campbell thought he knew what he ought to have said to the two men in the parlour car:

"We are to suspend judgment, not doubting either the Holy Scripture or the results of human observation and reasoning, but believing that it is possible, given sufficient knowledge and understanding, to reconcile the apparent contradiction."

But would even St. Augustine have convinced the blighters?

8

Bishop Campbell preached in Minneapolis, St. Paul, Los Angeles, Chicago, Pittsburgh, Allentown, Miami, Cincinnati, Delaware, Las Vegas, New Orleans, Baton Rouge, Dubuque, South Bend, Troy, Richmond, Washington, Seattle, Worcester, Fargo, Fond du Lac, Salt Lake City, and returned to the Acropolis and Parthenon in New York with $10,325.60 in his pocket. He was trying to unblock his basin with a nail file when the telephone rang:

"The name's Rooney. Monsignor Rooney. It was my nephew Pat that let those cigars through the Customs for you, and he didn't know then that you were a Bishop. Well, one good turn deserves another, that's what I say. What about having lunch with me today at the Waldorf-Astoria? One o'clock shall we say? I'll book the table."

"Thank you very much indeed, Monsignor. I'll be delighted." Here indeed was the charity which was not puffed up. Where else but in America would priests' nephews allow Pope's cigars through the Customs and then get their uncles to invite you to lunch as well?

"That's swell. I'm bringing along a bunch of the boys. They're sure excited at the thought of meeting up with a real live British Bishop."

As the Bishop had expected, Monsignor Rooney

had a Maynooth face, and the twelve huge priests he brought with him strode into the restaurant of the Waldorf-Astoria like the Notre Dame team taking the field at South Bend.

"Father O'Neill, Father Rocamare, Father Michou, Father Meynahems, Father Kasybeck, Father Grabowski, Father MacTavish, Father Kelly, Father Gretlein, Father da Samo, Father O'Toole, Father Meulemeester," the Monsignor said as he introduced the hairy he-man Universal Church. "Now where the hell's the maiter-dee? Oh, there you are, Gino. The Bishop of Missolongi's table, and I hope for your sake it's a good one."

How right the Bishop of Minnehaha had been, Bishop Campbell thought: the Church in America taught its sons manners as well as theology. Even in Rome itself a priest would not have thought of reserving a table in his guest's name out of respect for the hierarchy.

"Now, Bishop, which do you prefer?" Monsignor Rooney asked. "A martini or a manhattan?"

"A manhattan, please, Monsignor."

"Say, Bishop, is that right? One shouldn't put sugar in porridge?" Father O'Neill, Father Rocamare, Father Michou, Father Meynahems, Father Kasybeck, Father Grabowski, Father MacTavish, Father Kelly, Father Gretlein, Father da Samo, Father O'Toole or Father Meulemeester asked.

"Of course not; only salt," the Bishop answered,

and then saw that Father O'Neill, Father Rocamare, Father Michou, Father Meynahems, Father Kasybeck, Father Grabowski, Father MacTavish, Father Kelly, Father Gretlein, Father da Samo, Father O'Toole or Father Meulemeester wasn't listening but was shouting for a martini or a manhattan with the rest of the Universal Church.

" Make them real rigtail snorters," the Monsignor was telling the *maître d'hôtel*. " King size."

" Salt only," the Bishop said again; but by now Father O'Neill's, Father Rocamare's, Father Michou's, Father Meynahems's, Father Kasybeck's Father Grabowski's, Father MacTavish's, Father Kelly's, Father Gretlein's, Father da Samo's, Father O'Toole's or Father Meulemeester's face was stuck behind a menu the size of a recruiting poster.

When the Bishop had studied his own recruiting poster and ordered the only dishes he understood, the Universal Church was bawling at itself:

" They say that Spelly's a dead cert."

" ' You should go to Saint Eff Ex,' I said. 'It's very innaresting.' "

" What the hell they want to make a s.o.b. like him a Bishop for beats me."

" That'll all very well, but to be pious doesn't mean you've got to be wet assed."

" I think we could do with another of these each," the Monsignor told the waiter when he brought the drinks. " Our brother priests of the body," he told the Bishop, nodding at the ticketed men at the next table.

Their brother priests of the body were going at it hard too:

"Unfortunately the old cow could only pay a hundred bucks."

"I should have thought the insurance payments would have taken care of that."

"We routinely ordered him over for X-rays although he couldn't even belch properly."

"Can you show it will work on experimental animals?"

So as not to have to think about the experimental animals the Bishop tuned in on the Church Militant again:

"We're not in a position to co-ordinate our general expenses of course but fortunately the pastor's been in the accounting line."

"Barney Brannigan's just bought a Cadillac."

Bishop Campbell tried not to remember what his brother of Minnehaha had said about materialism. Weren't the brash faces just a little too confident? Wasn't it better that priests should look unhappy and hunted like the Abbé Bonpapa? "Persecution's not such a bad thing," he had once heard the Old Jock say. "It cleans clergymen like emery paper cleans cleeks." Was this the obverse of the crowded congregations: the good laity producing the trivial presbyters, the means of salvation degenerating into the means

to more means? Would the Curé of Ars have shouted
for double absinthes for himself and the Bishop of
Belley? Was it fitting that priests should sit and laugh
with other priests? Ought not every priest to be
alone with his attempt to obey God? At this very
moment children were dying of starvation and terrified
animals were being strapped down on operating
tables. Next to politicians' were not ecclesiastics'
grins the most fatuous? Lack of imagination was also
a sin.

" Now, Bishop, you choose," Monsignor Rooney
said as he handed Bishop Campbell the wine list.
" Don't be shy now. Make it sumpin' good. We've
been long enough on the water waggon in this
country."

A little out of practice since Monsignor Samson-
Slingsby had been made Vicar-General, the Bishop
chose the most expensive Montrachet he could find,
sure that the Archdiocese of New York could afford it.

" I guess we can go half a bottle each, Gino, so
you'd better bring us seven," Monsignor Rooney
said to the *maître d'hôtel*. " And now, Bishop,
what's your honest-to-God opinion of the Church
in America? Give us your spiel."

Thirteen attentive faces were turned towards the
Bishop. How unpardonably he had misjudged them,
the Bishop told himself, and gave them his thoughts
on the Form and the Spirit, and had them all still
listening until well after their second brandy.

" In other words," he concluded, " what you are doing here in North America is proof positive of Our Lord's promise to Peter that the gates of hell shall not prevail against the Church."

" Well, boys, I guess that's a hint for us to be beating it back to our parishes and hearing those first Friday confessions," Monsignor Rooney said as he rose and held out his hand. " 'Bye, Bishop, it's been swell seeing you."

" Everything's been just Jim Dandy," Father O'Neill said.

" We sure got a kick out of it, Bishop," Father Rocamare said.

" Thanks a lot," Father Michou said.

" You bet," Father Meynahems said.

" We're sure grateful to you, Bishop," Father Kasybeck said.

" Come again, Bishop," Father Grabowski said.

" You'll be welcome," Father MacTavish said.

" Yah," Father Kelly said.

" No kidding," Father Gretlein said.

" By Golly no," Father da Samo said.

" Be seeing you, Bishop," Father O'Toole said.

" And how!" Father Meulemeester said.

The check for the Universal Church's lunch came to $135.60; as he took out his pocket book to pay for it, the Bishop was sure that the Old Jock would laugh his head off.

9

But the Bishop was not to go home as soon as he expected.

That same afternoon the Apostolic Delegate summoned the Bishop to Washington and informed him of the Pope's desire that His Holiness's loyal son, the Lord Bishop of Missolongi, in the regions of the unfaithful, should proceed immediately to Spain and investigate an imprinting of the stigmata alleged to have occurred in a town called Menicarlo.

CHAPTER IX

"*Somos todos hermanos,*" the Archbishop of San Firmín de las Estrellas y Rio Largo said when he had sprinkled Bishop Campbell with holy water and censed him in the porch of his cathedral.

"His Most Illustrious Excellency asks me to tell His Illustrious Excellency that we are all brethren and sistern," the Archbishop's tubby chaplain translated.

"Please tell His Illustrious Excellency that it is a great honour for me to assist at High Mass in the country of Saint Teresa of Avila and Saint John of the Cross," Bishop Campbell answered.

To the wheeze of merry-go-round music the Bishop

was hustled into the sanctuary almost at the double and plumped down on a faldstool.

"*Deus, in adjutorium meum intende,*" a row of grinning baboons in knave-of-diamonds birettas and waisted cottas bawled at the orang outangs on the other side of the choir.

"*Domine, ad adjuvandum me festina,*" the orang outangs shouted back to the baboons.

The singing of the office cleaned the world, the Bishop remembered he had told Captain Inches. The song was more than the sum of the sounds which made it, and even this gabble was sucked into the spiral of meant praise rising from Quair, Caldey, Cassino, Fort Augustus and Gold Rush Gulch. But priests who rattled through rites bore the dreadful responsibility of appearing what their enemies imagined them to be: the hypocritical servants of reaction and obscurantism. The whole purpose of the liturgy was to make men so blind with God's beauty that they wouldn't see their neighbour's ugliness.

The empty-eyed celebrant, deacon and sub-deacon came bounding in and began the High Mass. During the *Gloria* they chatted together on the sedilia, the acolytes scratched themselves on the altar steps and His Most Illustrious Excellency picked his nose. At the consecration the Host was raised with one hand, and Bishop Campbell closed his eyes tight so as not to see what happened with the chalice. Apart from the Humpty Dumpty canons dozing in their stalls, the congregation consisted of three old women and a young man reading a newspaper, although there was a crowd round a side altar where an ancient parchmenty priest was galloping through a Low Mass in fourteen minutes. The Bishop had to tell himself very hard that one of the proofs of the Divine Origin of the Church was that the Holy Ghost had always prevented the most paltry of her anointed from talking the nonsense of the wise.

" *Entonces vamos a comer,*" the Archbishop said to Bishop Campbell as soon as the Canons had rushed them back into the sacristy.

" His Most Illustrious Excellency suggests to His Illustrious Excellency that they go together to the eating," the chaplain translated.

The Archbishop and Bishop Campbell were hustled out of the cathedral again and bundled into a waiting Rolls-Royce. The Canons pushed past the beggars and cripples in the porch and crammed into the two Daimlers behind. Two civil guards gave a slovenly salute and a woman with a rosary wrapped round her like a snow chain cheered.

" *Somos todos hermanos,*" the Archbishop said as he sketched a few hasty benedictions at a group of sullen gapers.

" His Most Illustrious Excellency is telling His Illustrious Excellency that we are all brethren and sistern," the chaplain translated.

" *Hermanos, si,*" Bishop Campbell repeated and,

noticing the scowls directed at his own and the
Archbishop's purple by the shabby men and women
watching on the pavement, wondered for how long.
Money was the measure of man's inability to love his
neighbour as himself, and it looked as though what
had happened to the Orthodox Church in Russia
might very well happen to the Catholic in Spain.

" *Me han dicho que el rey Jorge està en punto de hacerse
católico*," the Archbishop said.

" His Most Illustrious Excellency tells His Illustrious
Excellency that he had heard that King Georgie is
about to become a Kath Olic," the Chaplain translated.

" I think that His Most Illustrious Excellency has
been misinformed," Bishop Campbell answered.
" According to Dean Inge His Majesty's interest in
religion is confined to the prescription that clergymen
who preach before him should not wear moustaches."

" *Quién es Dean Inge?* "

" His Most Illustrious Excellency asks His Illustrious
Excellency who Dean Inge is."

" Dean Inge is a clergyman of the Established
Church of England who is also a writer."

" *Mas grande que Edgar Rice Burroughs?* "

" His Most Illustrious Excellency asks His Illustrious
Excellency whether Dean Inge is a greater writer
than Edgar Rice Burroughs. His Most Illustrious
Excellency derived much enjoyment from his perusal
of *Tarzan of the Apes*."

" *Para venir a saberlo todo*
No quieras algo saber en nada . . ."

Bishop Campbell remembered from St. John of the
Cross. Was Ethel M. Dell also a way of know-
ing nothing, and P. C. Wren of ascending Mount
Carmel?

" The Holy Father is very interested in the miracle
which has just taken place in Your Most Illustrious
Excellency's Archdiocese," he said.

The Archbishop shrugged his shoulders and
mumbled something which Bishop Campbell did not
catch.

" His Most Illustrious Excellency asks His Illustrious
Excellency whether it is true that His Holiness has
granted a private audience to the glorious writer
Edgar Rice Burroughs," the chaplain translated.

The Bishop gave up.

2

" *Somos todos hermanos*," the Archbishop said as he
shovelled on to his plate almost all the salmon on the
dish held out to him by the flunkey.

" His Most Illustrious Excellency tells His Illustrious
Excellency that we are all brethren and sistern," the
chaplain translated with a dismayed eye on what still
remained of the fish.

There was consternation on the other faces round the

table too, the Bishop saw, and then noticed that, with the Archbishop's, the chaplain's and his own, there were thirteen of them. Although superstition had been condemned by the Church he was uneasy: the Archbishop, his chaplain and the big-jowled Canons looked far too fat to be in danger of dying within a year.

"Padre Todo o Nada will drive you down to Menicarlo on Friday, Your Excellency," the Archbishop said, nodding across the table at the chaplain, who was too busy scouring the fish dish to translate. "Indeed it's because of his driving that we call him 'All or Nothing.' Your Excellency would understand why if you'd seen the way he charged at the crowd coming out of the bullfight on the Feast of the Annunciation."

At once Bishop Campbell was so miserable that he scarcely noticed the second dish of salmon which had arrived to relieve the Canons' anxiety. Politeness was a form of charity, but would he not be sinning from motives of human respect if he allowed those laughing fools to imagine that he connived at cruelty? What sort of priests were they who imagined that the Mother of God could be honoured by disembowelling horses and sticking spikes into bulls?

"His Most Illustrious Excellency says that he thinks he can see from His Illustrious Excellency's expression His Illustrious Excellency does not approve of our national Spanish sport."

The barely concealed mockery on the thick faces made the Bishop tremble with hurt and anger.

" Tell His Most Illustrious Excellency," he snapped, " that if His Most Illustrious Excellency will read the Encyclical *De Gregis Salute* of 1565 he will see that His Holiness St. Pius V didn't approve of it either."

" His Most Illustrious Excellency says that if His Illustrious Excellency will reread the Encyclical in question His Illustrious Excellency will find that His Holiness St. Pius V condemned bullfighting, not because of the cruelty to the bull, but only because the cruelty to the bull might blunt the spectators' sensibilities and make them cruel to their fellow men. His Most Illustrious Excellency would point out to His Illustrious Excellency that this danger has now passed and so the Encyclical has become a dead letter."

It was Monsignor Samson-Slingsby and Father Ricaby all over again.

" Not in the opinion of people with any heart at all, it hasn't." The Bishop looked round the table for a sign of pity on one single guzzling face, but the cold eyes were as empty of clemency as shell fish. " And if His Most Illustrious Excellency had had any experience of modern warfare he might realise that the danger of which His Most Illustrious Excellency speaks is still very much with us."

" His Most Illustrious Excellency is of the opinion

that animals were made for man and not man for animals. His Most Illustrious Excellency is also of the opinion that bullfighting is a Catholic art."

"Please tell His Most Illustrious Excellency from me that if I thought that for one moment I'd become a Protestant again tomorrow."

The Bishop was by now far too angry to be worried by the shocked silence. 75% of humanity was stupid, 75% wicked and the other two 25%'s never coincided, Cardinal Bourne had told the Old Jock in 1907: the Spanish clergy seemed to be in both 75%'s. Here indeed was Form mouldering for want of Spirit. These gabblers of the Mysteries could love neither God nor their neighbour. Why were the compulsorily chaste always so much more merciless than the lechers? The least mournful faces at funerals were always those of the clergy, and they generally had less reason than the laity for hoping that the deceased could be saved. Once again the Bishop found himself wishing that souls might transmigrate after death, and that one day a Most Illustrious Excellency maddened by banderillas might ram his horns into the bowels of a Reverendo Todo o Nada.

"His Most Illustrious Excellency thinks that His Illustrious Excellency is under a misapprehension," the chaplain was saying. "His Most Illustrious Excellency wishes to draw His Illustrious Excellency's attention to the fact that the horses have their vocal chords cut before they enter the bullring so that their shrieks may not distress the more impressionable among the spectators."

" Faith that knows no doubt is dead," Unamuno had written. Was it because they read only Edgar Rice Burroughs that these fools were able to go on believing uncritically? Was it because they had never heard of Bertrand Russell that their charity wasn't even the precaution of not being unkind to others in case others should be unkind to them?

The Bishop was almost glad when he began to be frightened again about their having sat down thirteen to table.

3

" More like the moon than the earth," Belloc had written of Spain, but Padre Todo o Nada hurtled his car too quickly over the potholes for the Bishop to do more than see that the leaves of the olive trees were silver with sunlight when he bounced. Had sitting down thirteen to table got left out of the Scriptures as well as the transmigration of souls? The Bishop was inclined to think so when the chaplain told him that he had passed his driving test only because the examiner hadn't known that the instructor sitting beside Padre Todo o Nada had been operating the dual controls.

Past flocks of goats on dried-up river beds, under green fountains of palms, past horsemen on Rosinante, they tore through villages, scattering hens and

Muscovy ducks. Pedestrians were a danger for motorists, Padre Todo o Nada told the Bishop as he swerved round old women gossiping in the middle of a street, and at night nuns ought to be compelled to wear tail lights.

The Bishop was clinging in terror to the door when they shot in between the white and yellow houses of Menicarlo; and there, at three o'clock precisely, he saw the wounds of Christ's Passion open on the body of Pepita Gutierrez, and he knew that God's arm was still round the Church, to protect it from clergymen who liked bullfights.

CHAPTER X

As HE mounted the steps of St. Peter's the Bishop caught himself thinking into the heads of the seminarians the thoughts he himself had had when he was young. In a side chapel the holy old boys were fuddling through the liturgy, and at the font babies were queueing for the chance of becoming saints. The Bishop knelt and said a prayer for Christ's rickety Church throughout the world, and then went round to the Cortile di San Damaso where he had an appointment with Monsignor Pantachini.

There could be no doubt at all about the authenticity of the miracle of Menicarlo, the Bishop said. Autosuggestion was ruled out, as it had not been Pepita Gutierrez's hands but her wrists which had been pierced, and the girl was unlikely to have known that it was through them and not through Our Lord's palms that the Roman soldiers had driven the nails. The Bishop himself and the Archbishop's chaplain had been alone with the girl both when the wounds had opened on the Friday and closed again on the Sunday, so there had been no possibility of trickery.

"Between you and me, there are times when I can't make Our Lord out," Monsignor Pantachini said. "'An evil and an adulterous generation seeketh after a sign,' He said, and He keeps on sending them: a crucifix answering Mass in Naples last week and another crop of roses round a statue in Stockton-on-Tees. One would almost think He wanted to convert us!"

"It mightn't be such a bad idea," the Bishop said, managing a smile. "At present most people's religion boils down to the not very confident reiteration of their fathers' guess at the transcendental."

"Kerygmatic catechesis is the answer to that, my Lord. According to Monsignor Wumerumbani of the Gold Coast at least. Revive kerygmatic catechesis, he says, and jockeys will start discussing theology in night clubs.

"One doesn't argue about God only with one's mouth, Monsignor. Will kerygmatic catechesis make

Spanish priests observe the rubrics? Encyclicals don't seem to have done much good."

" Give them time, my Lord, give them time. After all it's only two hundred years since we called them to order."

" And bullfights? " the Bishop asked bitterly. " Or is four hundred years still too little? "

2

" Perhaps the letter which I shall send your Archbishop yesterday will alluminate the meanings of the matter," the Pope said as he raised Bishop Campbell from his knees. "Believe me, I am as sickly tired of cruel men and lazyboned priests as is Your Excellency but even in this 'oly place I must shake hands with Say Ten many times a day. And now perhaps Your Excellency will be kind enough to stand backwards formost with me."

Surprised, Bishop Campbell did as the Pope had asked, and felt on his head the Fisherman's Ring.

" Bishops should not ought to be big men," the Pope said as he turned the Bishop round to face him again. " *Mi vogliono bene perchè sono piccolo.* They are putting up with me because I am a small one. Bye-bye, Your Excellency. I must be shaking hands again with Say Ten."

CHAPTER XI

" You're looking very well fed, my Lord," Monsignor Samson-Slingsby said when he greeted Bishop Campbell on his return, and then led him upstairs to the room in which the one hundred and twenty-seventh Archbishop of Inchkeith and the Pentlands lay dying.

" Go, Christian soul, from this world . . ." Father O'Leary's peaky little consecrated bus conductor's face was praying above the rattle of roller skates in the streets below. With his Canons around him on their knees, Moncrieff of Abernuthie, Stuart of Minloch, Kilgour of Braetosh, Baird of Kinlochree, the Archbishop was ending his religious life as he had begun it, in his slum cathedral parish, to the seeping smell of fish and chips.

" Pneumonia," the Monsignor whispered to the Bishop.

On the bed the Old Jock was rambling:

" I've never been a mystic. ' Wagner and boiled mutton,' Belloc called the Dark Night of the Soul. ' The Customs of the Matter,' Huxley called God. I'd rather make an act of contrition to a bowler hat."

The Bishop remembered having once seen the

Vicar-General insist on finishing a cigar before going into church to bury a girl of three, but today the Monsignor was as near sobbing as the rest.

" Would you believe it? St. Francis of Assisi asked for marzipan on his death bed," the Archbishop said.

". . . . in the name of angels and archangels," Father O'Leary prayed, " in the name of thrones and dominions; in the name of principalities and powers; in the name of virtues, Cherubim and Seraphim . . ."

" Johnny Knox wasn't as wrong as all that: ' the Kirk is knawen onelie to God.' " The Archbishop's eyes shone blue at Bishop Campbell, and the Bishop went close to the bed and took the old man's hand.

". . . in the name of holy martyrs and confessors; in the name of holy monks and hermits . . ."

" Sometimes you'll find it a bit cauld up on top, laddie," the Archbishop told Bishop Campbell before he died.

2

Bishop Campbell sang the requiem from the faldstool. " *Te decet hymnus in Sion et tibi reddet votum in Jerusalem,*" he read from the missal held up to his face.

The sanctuary was purple with prelates and the front pews crammed with all the big unbelievers from the Town Council, the University Senate and the

Fire Brigade. Behind them scepticism tapered away
into faith, via the Episcopal Dean and the Minister
of the High Kirk to the hugger mugger of old rag
and bone women in their husbands' caps at the back.

" *In momento, in ictu oculi, in novissima tuba*," sang
the sub-deacon. " *Canet enim tuba, et mortui resurgent
incorrupti: et nos immutabimur.*"

Then came Monsignor Samson-Slingsby's
panegyric:

" We are gathered today in this beautiful cathedral
church to do homage to our venerated Archbishop
who is now enjoying the eternal felicity he has so
richly earned."

When, the Bishop wondered, would the clergy
learn not to mix feeling with rhetoric? When would
they learn to tell the truth? The pro-cathedral was
plain down-right ugly and the Old Jock himself
would have been the first to admit that he required a
twinge or two of privation before he was fit to see
God. The Bishop was glad to get on again with the
strong words which the Church had laid out against
the stupidity of her priests, and to pray that, in the
abundance of the Lord's mercies, John, His Bishop,
might be united with Him for ever.

The five absolutions were given by their Lordships
of Hawick, Tobermory, Glentulchan, Madrid-Alcalà
and Cracow. The coffin was borne through streets
lined with charwomen, labourers, sailors and prostitutes. The Bishop of Hexham and Newcastle recited

the prayers of committal, Campbell as well as Mac-Donald pipes played the Flowers of the Forest, and Bishop Campbell thought how amused the Old Jock would have been about the bill for the Universal Church's lunch.

CHAPTER XII

ARCHBISHOP CAMPBELL found it "cauld up on top" all right.

To begin with there was the lack of money: it was difficult to run ninety-two parishes on the voluntary contributions of tram drivers, billiard-markers and Irish maids, even with the bookmakers and publicans to help them. When the expenses of the Old Jock's funeral and his own enthronement had been paid for, the balance at the Union Bank of Scotland had sunk to seventy-six pounds. Cardinal Wiseman had tried to provide every priest in England and Wales with a salary of fifty pounds a year; the Archbishop of Inchkeith and the Pentlands was lucky when he could make it forty.

The Archbishop crumpled the paper on which he had made his calculations and threw it on the floor for Tartan Tom to play with.

The Vicar-General entered without knocking.

"That blasted cat," he said, sidestepping hurriedly.

"Father Chisholm's been on the telephone, Your Grace. He's fallen off his bicycle and hurt his left arm and wonders if he can wear his maniple on his right."

"Tell him to leave it off altogether until his left arm gets better."

"But, Your Grace, the Sacred Congregation of Rites . . ."

"In this Archdiocese, Monsignor, I am the Sacred Congregation of Rites." It wasn't true of course and only confusion could result if every Ordinary were to take it into his head to decide about rubrics on his own, but the Archbishop was in no mood to be gentle with the Vicar-General who, in spite of his new two-seater Vauxhall and his Spalding Midgets, held out his hand at the end of the month like everybody else. "In case you don't know it takes two hundred years to get a liturgical decision out of Rome and Father Chisholm's arm ought to be better long before that." This wasn't quite the way Miss Assisi had put it, but the Archbishop had long given up being scrupulous about the kind of stick he used to beat down the Monsignor's pride with.

"Father Walsh has written in to ask whether the taking of snuff breaks the eucharistic fast."

"Smoking doesn't. So why should snuff? But it's a filthy habit. Tell him to use his common sense." Remembering how St. Thérèse of Lisieux had struggled to overcome her impatience with the nun next to her in chapel who clicked her rosary too loudly, the Archbishop worked up a smile for the Vicar-General's Vat 69 face. " All right, Monsignor. Next for shaving."

" Father Brodie's been at it again, Your Grace. He rang up the holy hens at Glenlady and pretended to be the Cardinal Patriarch of Lisbon and told them they could gain a plenary indulgence if they recited the rosary at noon every day for a week for the intentions of St. Vigo of Baixo-Alemetejo. The blighter would have got away with it too had the Reverend Ma not happened to know that there's no St. Vigo of Baixo-Alemetejo."

" I'll deal with Father Brodie myself. He's the one that's always grinning in choir, isn't he? And that reminds me, Monsignor. My compliments to the cathedral clergy and tell them that this smirking at one another across the chancel has got to stop. It doesn't happen in Cologne or Rheims and it's not going to happen in St. Bean's. From now on every parade will be a colonel's parade, except when I'm away visiting or confirming High Mass on Sunday with sung *coram arciepiscopo*. It'll be time enough for Father Brodie and his friends to start grinning when they've converted Scotland. Tell them the least they can do to atone for their inefficiency is to look humble during the celebration of the Mysteries."

" Very good, Your Grace. I'll tell them." But behind the enamel of his obedience the Archbishop could imagine the Vicar-General preparing: " Heard the latest, boys? His Nibs wants us to behave at High Mass like a lot of bloody Protestants in the House of Rimmon."

" Anything else, Monsignor? "

" Your Grace's Lenten pastoral. Which are you going to shoot at? The Thistle or the Scratcher? " The Scratcher was a 2/6 Scratcher now, with private boxes at 3/9 for couples. " His Holiness has given us a lead there, I think. There's not much ' *Casti Connubii* ' in one or the other."

" ' Teach us to observe the teachings of St. Obesimus on purity, certain of which were infallible.' I've had enough of directing polysyllabic prudences at the usual sitting ducks of drunkenness and fornication."

" Marriage has to be a Sacrament, Your Grace, if only to make laymen stick to the dreadful women they once thought they would like to get into bed with for ever." The telephone on the Archbishop's desk rang, and Monsignor Samson-Slingsby answered tonily: " Vicar-General Inchkeith and the Pentlands. No, Mrs. Stair-Graham. Three Persons in one God, not one Person in Three Gods. Not at all. Tell the General I'll be waiting for him in the club house at three o'clock on Thursday." The *bonhomie* peeled off the Vicar-General's face as he laid down the receiver. " Why the hell those old trout can't look up Athanasius for themselves beats me. Yes, Your Grace, you were saying? "

" *You* were saying, Monsignor; *I* wasn't." Knowing that it was no longer any use trying to get out of showing the Vicar-General the draft of his pastoral, the Archbishop took it out of a drawer and handed it across the desk.

" ' *Trahison des laics*,' they'll never get that," the Vicar-General said as soon as he had read the first few words. " Why, most of them have never even heard of the ' *trahison des clercs*.' I know what Your Grace is getting at of course: the Church not only consisting of the clergy but of the vast unco-operative porridge of the laity as well and that it is they who have forced us to lower our standards in the hope of wheedling them into saving their unfortunately immortal souls."

After that bright firework the phrases which had pleased the Archbishop most seemed tame when the Vicar-General read them out:

" It is the mystery about God that is certain and the certainty about man that is mysterious."

" Worship has to be public in order to make the weak imagine they are strong."

" I don't altogether know that I like that pun about holiness and wholeness; and a semi-colon after ' transcendental,' wouldn't you say ? " Monsignor Samson-Slingsby handed the Archbishop back his pastoral as though it were a bedpan. " Anyway I still think Your Grace would have done much better to stick to something good and wholesome like adultery."

The Archbishop scarcely heard: putting his typescript back in the drawer, he had noticed the date on the calendar: TUESDAY 12th FEBRUARY 1935; and it had been on SUNDAY 11th FEBRUARY 1934 that he had sat down thirteen to lunch with His Most Illustrious Excellency of San Firmín de las Estrellas y Rio Largo. The year was up. If death had struck anybody it had not struck him. Had Padre Todo o Nada at last paid the penalty for his reckless driving? The Archbishop tried to atone both for his relief and his superstition by not biting back at the Vicar-General.

" *Tot homines, tot sententiae*, Monsignor."

" Quite, Your Grace; but wasn't it precisely so that there should be only one opinion for all mankind that Our Lord founded the Church on Peter? "

" I agree, Monsignor. But we must distinguish between opinions about truths which have been revealed to us and opinions about matters at whose nature we can only guess. Hell for example. Does it consist in flames or eternal regret? "

" My bet's flames, Your Grace, and plenty of them."

As soon as the Vicar-General had left him the Archbishop went up to his bedroom. He had changed nothing in it since it had been the Old Jock's: the iron bedstead was the same, the chipped china ewer and basin, the washstand with the varnish flaking off. Untying the knot in order to tighten the string wrapped round the door of the wardrobe to hold the mirror in its socket, the Archbishop was startled by a knock at the door and let go.

" Seven years' bad luck, the superstitious would say," the Vicar-General said as he helped the Archbishop to pick up the bits of broken glass. " Your Grace hasn't got any slithers of soap he doesn't want by any chance. As usual I'm on the scrounge for stickers."

CHAPTER XIII

USUALLY, THE Archbishop thought, it took a minute for a preacher's stupidity to show through. The visiting Canon's took ten seconds, and the man had had every chance too, because Father O'Leary had given out the notices for him, and read the gospel for the day in English, all about Jechonias having begot Salathiel, and Salathiel Zorobabel, and Zorobabel Abiud.

" Every morning when we open our eyes and see the bonnie purple heather blooming on the distant hills our hearts are filled with gratitude to Almighty God for nature's superabundant proof of His goodness."

Had the fool never heard of stoats fastening on the throats of terrified rabbits? Didn't the nincompoop know that in spite of Sir Harry Lauder colour was an illusion caused by the retina's refraction of light?

It was Sunday 8th September 1935, the Feast of the Nativity of the Blessed Virgin, and, high on his throne between his master of ceremonies, deacon and sub-deacon, the Archbishop, gloved hands palm downwards on the *gremiale*, couldn't get out of listening.

" And when we go to the seaside, my dear brethren in Jesus Christ, and hear the happy laughter of the bairns as they gambol on the sands . . ."

Was this part of his seven years' bad luck for having broken that mirror? Hadn't Hitler and Mussolini and shortage of money to finish the Old Jock's sanctuary been enough?

" And when we listen to the birds in the trees greeting each new day with their *Sursum Corda* . . ."

Of one thing the Archbishop was sure: it wouldn't be the worms that answered: " *Habemus ad Dominum.*"

And yet was he being unjust?

" Glory be to God for dappled things," Father Gerard Manley Hopkins had written; and " Cuckoo-echoing, bell-swarmèd, lark-charmèd, rook-racked, river-rounded." Had even the Jesuit been unaware of the " aboriginal catastrophe? "

" Indeed we can say that the Most Glorious and Indivisible Trinity is the only true Royal Academician."

The Canon carved a huge cross over the dozing

congregation, came down from the pulpit and carried his dull face cockily up between the bowing choir and knelt before the throne for a blessing.

With his problem still unsolved, the Archbishop rose and began the Creed.

2

NOMEN ARCIEPISCOPI:
DONALDUS

the reminder in the sacristy for the *Te Igitur* ran these days, but the Archbishop never passed without saying a prayer for Joannis, whose portrait now hung at the end of the line of his predecessors and the misty Vicars Apostolic.

By their Sunday newspapers shall ye know them, the Archbishop thought as he went into the common-room: the Vicar-General was reading the *Observer*, Father O'Leary the *Sunday Express*, Father Veitch the *Sunday Dispatch*, Father Brodie the *News of the World* and the visiting Canon the *Catholic Trumpet*.

French anxiety was growing, the *Sunday Times* said; Mussolini had Appealed to the British People and Japan had Warned them; Miss Denise Robins had published *Life and Love*, a man called Graham Greene *England Made Me*, and the Mode this Season was going to Depend on Clever Corsetry.

" Would you believe it now, Your Grace? " Father

Brodie said. "It asks here: 'Has the Church Missed the Bus?'"

"It means the Protestant Church, ye gowk," Father O'Leary said.

"It's the bus that's missed the Church if you ask me," the Vicar-General said. "Now, Your Grace, what do you think of this? 'God is not a name but a concept. Is this perhaps the reason that His *essentia involvit existentiam?*'"

"Who spilled that one, Monsignor?" Father Brodie asked. "Gracie Fields?"

"Another crack like that, Father, and you'll be on the six ack emma confessions every day for a month." The Vicar-General turned earnestly back to the Archbishop. "'To believe means precisely that dialectical hovering which, although in fear and trembling, never despairs. Faith is an infinite self-made care as to whether one has faith—and that self-made care is faith.'"

"That's rather like Gerard Manley Hopkins," the Archbishop said, pleased to be able to think of the Jesuit poet again.

"'Thou are indeed just, Lord, if I contend
    With thee; but, sir, so what I plead is just.
    Why do sinners' ways prosper? and why must
    Disappointment all I endeavour end?'"

"I think you've missed the point, Your Grace," the Vicar-General said acidly. "Hopkins was just spewing up the Psalms again; all that ungodly-flourishing-like-the-green-bay-tree bilge. Kierkegaard is original. So much so that he's going to make me have to re-write half of *Freewill and the Molecule.* ' The supreme paradox of all thought is the attempt to discover something which thought cannot think.' Gerard M. could never have said a thing like that for all he was a holy J."

> " ' Wild air, world-mothering air,
> Nestling me everywhere?'

Could your Gaardekierk have said a thing about Our Lady like that?"

" *Kierkegaard.* Kierkegaard happened to be a Danish Protestant, Your Grace, but I think that the Mother of God herself must have been the first to forgive him when she found out that he had said ' The self is doubly dialectical.' "

" All the same, if the man was a Protestant . . ." the visiting Canon said.

" ' In religion as in politics the pendulum always swings too far: from the barbarities of the Aztec sacrifice to no sacrifice at all,' " the Vicar-General said. " And this time that's not Kierkegaard, Canon; it's me."

The Archbishop was glad when the gong sounded for lunch.

" I think Your Grace will find that it's got body."

Monsignor Samson-Slingsby said as he elaborately sipped a drop from the bottle of *Clos Vougeot* which he had had brought up from the cellar for the Archbishop, the visiting Canon and himself.

"Tartan Tom again," Father Brodie said as he raised his glass of beer to Father Veitch.

The Archbishop pretended to be listening only to what the visiting Canon was saying to the Vicar-General:

"If you want my honest opinion, Monsignor, all those so-called atrocities in the German concentration camps have been greatly exaggerated."

All the Archbishop's impatience with the Canon's stupid sermon returned, and anger rocked his protest;

"On the contrary, Canon, I have it from the Cardinal Archbishop of Cologne himself that what we've been told is only a fraction of the horrible truth."

The Canon emptied his wine glass into a mouth jammed tight with chicken and roast potato.

"Anyway, Your Grace, the Jews have brought it on themselves."

"And the Abyssinians, Canon? Have they brought it on themselves too?"

"No doubt Mussolini has his reasons, Your Grace. And the Italian Bishops seem to be backing him too. Throwing their episcopal rings into the melting pot they are."

"Then the fools are playing Hitler's game and not God's." Grief rather than anger was now making the Archbishop's voice shake.

"Take it from me, Your Grace, Hitler and Mussolini will never come to anything. As far as we're likely to be concerned they're all my eye and Betty Martin."

"And as far as you're concerned, Canon, that's all that matters, is it?"

"I wonder if any of you know the origin of the phrase 'all my eye and Betty Martin,'" the Vicar-General said. "It's a Lancashire corruption of '*Ora pro mihi, beate Martine.*'"

"Sounds better than beer," Father Brodie said.

But the Archbishop was not going to be diverted from rebuking this fat priest who was brave about other people's sufferings. He knew what he wanted to say and he said it, straight into the Canon's cold eyes floating like oysters behind his steel-rimmed spectacles:

"All crimes committed by Catholics are not virtues, Canon, and all virtues practised by Jews are not crimes. If we don't realise that, other people do and they'll never listen to our doctrine until they see that our charity is at least as great as theirs. And if priests who sit in confessionals and shrive other people's sins don't understand elementary mercy and pity we can pray until we're blue in the face for the conversion of Scotland."

" ' Where'er a Catholic sun doth shine, there's always laughter and good red wine,' " Father Brodie quoted. " Anyway one thing's certain: we'll never get anywhere on beer."

CHAPTER XIV

THE CANONS' MASS on the first Tuesday of the month was always a red one, to invoke Divine Guidance upon their chapter meeting.

" O God," Canon Baird sang on the sixth of October 1936, " Who hast taught the hearts of the faithful by the light of the Holy Ghost, grant that, by the gift of the same Spirit, we may always be truly wise, and ever rejoice in His holy consolations."

Kneeling at the back of the empty cathedral, the Archbishop was shocked to notice the perpetual chewing movement of the Vicar-General's jaws. Monsignor Samson-Slingsby had been getting slack lately and so far the Archbishop had refrained from pulling him up because of his age. But even the oldest and most venerable Protonotary Apostolic couldn't expect to get away with Spearmint in choir. The Archbishop looked again. There could be no doubt about it: the Vicar-General's chin was pounding up and down like a threshing machine, and it was still doing so when the sacred ministers and their servers left the sanctuary and the Canons began to sing sext.

Part of the Chapters' business that morning was the allocation of the 1937 Forty Hours Devotion among the different churches of the Archdiocese and in the afternoon the Vicar-General came and told the Archbishop about the Canons' proposals.

" I'm still not altogether satisfied about the conduct of clergy in choir, Monsignor." The Archbishop, who was still more frightened of the Vicar-General than he liked to admit to himself, had decided to lead up to his rebuke gently. " Last Sunday evening when Father Brodie was preaching about the importance of praying for the grace of a happy death I noticed that both Father Veitch and Father O'Leary had their noses stuck in their breviaries."

" I don't think you can blame them for that, Your Grace. It's old hat as far as they're concerned: they know all about it already."

" Nobody knows all about it already, Monsignor. Meditation on the four last things never did the holiest of us any harm. Death, judgment, heaven, hell, nobody can think too much about them. St. Ignatius knew that if Fathers Veitch and O'Leary don't. Besides it's bad manners and risks putting Father Brodie off his stride."

" Nothing could ever put Father Brodie off his stride. Anyway he did the same thing to me when I was preaching about the only way of proving the existence of God being to refrain from trying to prove it and you can't say that even St. Ignatius knew anything about that."

" Anyway it's got to stop." Who would rid him of this turbulent priest?

" Of course, Your Grace, if you say so it will. But all the same I should like to point out that the Sacred Congregation of Rites has never laid anything down about priests not reading their breviaries during other priests' sermons."

" And chewing gum, Monsignor. As far as I know the Sacred Congregation of Rites hasn't given a ruling on that either, but it can scarcely be called a fitting way of honouring the Presence of Our Blessed Lord in the Eucharist. There's no use trying to get out of it, Monsignor. I was watching you this morning: your teeth were hard at it from the epistle to the last gospel."

The Archbishop was glad to have got his rebuke in while he was still angry.

" My *false* teeth, Your Grace. I've just got a new set and I'm afraid it'll be some little time before they work themselves in, but I'll make a point of wearing my old set in choir if that would please Your Grace better."

The Archbishop was horrified by his *gaffe* and too grateful to the Vicar-General for not laughing to be able to do so himself, even self-deprecatingly.

" I'm terribly sorry, Monsignor," he said. " Really,

I am. I ought to have known better. I can't think how I can have been so stupid. Forgive me, please do. I've been letting my zeal run away with me, I'm afraid. If you're kind you'll blame the Civil War in Spain."

"It's nothing, Your Grace. After all it's the sort of mistake anyone could have made. But the Civil War in Spain. I'm afraid I don't quite see what that's got to do with it."

The Archbishop snatched at this opportunity to change the subject.

"Why do you think the Guards fight better than other regiments?" he asked. "Because they drill better than other regiments. And priests who pay attention to rubrics pray better than priests who don't. I for one am convinced that this war in Spain would never have taken place if the clergy there hadn't been so abominably careless."

"The clergy, Your Grace. The clergy had nothing to do with it all. It's the hatred of God that's at the bottom of it all."

"Are you so sure, Monsignor? If you haven't seen the way Spanish priests say Mass, I have."

"The Cardinal Archbishop of Toledo must have seen them say Mass too, Your Grace, and he says Franco's cannons are the voice of the Gospel."

"That's just about the sort of stupid remark a Cardinal Primate would make."

At once they were at it again, hammer and tongs:

" As far as I am concerned, Your Grace, the civil war in Spain is a war between the powers of darkness and the powers of light, and only scoundrels like the French and fools like the British could think otherwise."

" How can cannons ever be the voice of a gospel which tells us to turn the other cheek and to walk two miles when we are asked to walk one? No, Monsignor, neither Franco's cannons with two n's nor his canons with one are the voice of the Gospel and still less his Cardinals."

" And the Russians, Your Grace? What are they doing in Barcelona and Madrid? Campaigning for family prayers in every Catholic home?"

" You're forgetting Hitler and Mussolini, aren't you?"

" And the burning of the churches, Your Grace. And the digging up dead nuns and exposing their bodies in the street? That's a form of Catholic Action, I suppose?"

" I don't think you quite understand, Monsignor. People have got to have a real reason for hating religion before they start setting fire to churches and murdering priests. The priests have always been on the side of the landowners and the extortioners. Our Lord didn't come down from heaven solely in order to save upper class cads."

" At least the upper classes know how to be cads like gentlemen."

But the Archbishop was much too angry to be in the mood for epigrams.

" Not in Newman's sense of the word, they don't. Don't let's fool ourselves, Monsignor. People always know when we're carrying out Christ's commands or merely preaching them. Even atheists allow priests to love God when they are seen to love their neighbour as well. The Spanish clergy weren't very good at either."

The Vicar-General walked huffily to the door.

" Your Grace asked me to remind him that he has a confirmation at St. Dympna's at five o'clock," he said and went out.

The four o'clock post brought a letter from Miss Assisi: rather than recant, Monsignor Pantachini said, the Archbishop and Cathedral Chapter of San Firmín de las Estrellas y Rio Largo had chosen to be stripped naked and dashed from a high cliff on to rocks.

" *Somos todos hermanos*," the Archbishop murmured as he knelt and prayed for His Most Illustrious Excellency, and then went and apologised to the Vicar-General.

2

The Archbishop had sold the Morris Minor after the Old Jock's death, and he travelled to St. Dympna's by tram.

Clergymen who kicked with the left foot were

still not popular in the city and when the Archbishop took out his breviary the blue-nosed woman on his left rose and went and sat opposite, next two unspiritual looking men in Teddy Bear overcoats.

"*Non accedet ad te malum: et flagellum non appropinquabit tabernaculo tuo,*" the Archbishop murmured.

"Jack told me at lunch today that he thought Luna Park hadn't got an earthly," one of the men in Teddy Bear overcoats said.

"He's talking through his hat, old man. Why, I've seen him jump off the ground all four legs at once."

Didn't the fools understand what was happening in Spain, the Archbishop wondered. Perhaps that was why so many people were reconciled to the Church only on their death-beds: when people were so careless of worldly danger they were unlikely to be perturbed by the thought of distant apocalyptic commotion.

"And how is infallibility this autumnal afternoon, Your Grace?"

The Archbishop looked up and saw that the seat vacated by the blue-nosed woman had been taken by the Episcopal Dean.

"And Spain?" the Dean went on. "Spin, span, spun and still spinning. What's His Holiness's answer to that one?"

The Archbishop smiled bravely.

" Even Your Grace can't deny that these unshaven Iberian obscurantists had it coming to them."

" I can and I do." For the second time that afternoon the Archbishop was so angry that he could scarcely speak. Would the Dean, he wondered, have been thrown from the top of the Walter Scott monument in Edinburgh in defence of the Thirty-Nine Articles?

" Now, now, Your Grace must know as well as I do that what the Church of Spain is most in need of is a breath of fresh air."

" The Church *in* Spain, you mean. It's only Britain that is stupid enough to imagine that God can reveal His truth exclusively to a particular country."

" Anyway you wouldn't find even Communists murdering clergymen of the Episcopal Church *in* Scotland."

" Of course not. They wouldn't bother. They attack professionals not amateurs. The struggle that is coming upon the world is between militant atheism and Catholic Christianity. Stalin knows he's got nothing to fear from croquet and pink iced cakes on the vicarage lawn."

As soon as he said this, the Archbishop was sorry, because he knew that the Dean was in good faith and that behind his asinine smirk lay a soul sore with other men's lack of love; but before he could apologise the Dean had smacked back:

" Anyway thank God I'm a Protestant."

"Last time I met you you were an Evangelical Catholic and if that isn't running with the hare and hunting with the hounds I'd very much like to know what is."

"I'm on your side, Your Grace," an old man sitting farther along from them said. "I'm a member of the One True Church too. Why, I was committing mortal sin long before Your Grace was even baptised."

Even the woman with the blue nose laughed, but the Dean was still looking hurt when he got off at the next stop but one. The Archbishop sat on feeling ashamed of his outburst. Twice within the space of a few hours he had lost his temper in an argument and tried to wound his opponent. Was this the best use he could make of the Holy Ghost which he had received *ad robur* when the Old Jock had ordained him a deacon? "*Quoniam angelis suis mandavit de te: qui custodiant te in omnibus viis tuis,*" he read on in his breviary, trying to forget his unworthiness.

The dentist who had attended the convent at East Hadwick was examining the nuns' teeth when the Archbishop arrived at St. Dympna's, and Reverend Mother insisted on His Grace having one on the house.

"That eye tooth of yours is a bit wobbly, Your Grace," the dentist told the Archbishop. "Three years I give it. Ten if you'll let me make you a bridge."

This time however the Holy Ghost *ad robur* worked, and the Archbishop did not remind the dentist that he had made the same prophecy to him ten years ago; and when he went into the chapel he prayed that the little girls he was going to confirm would turn out wiser, humbler and better tempered than himself.

CHAPTER XV

In April 1940 the Archbishop was invited by the Metropolitan Chapter of Notre Dame to give one of the five absolutions at Cardinal Verdier's funeral. The Abbé Bonpapa met him at the Gare du Nord at midnight, and as there were no taxis running they set out on foot for the *Archevêché*, taking it in turn to carry the Archbishop's suitcase.

" Anyway the old boy's chosen the right moment to die," the Abbé said as they clopped along together through the empty blacked-out streets. " The war's beginning in earnest now and Norway and Denmark won't be the only places to get it in the neck. If you ask me France is going to suffer as she has never suffered before. And what's more she'll have deserved it. Not only are Frenchmen no longer Christians: these days they're no longer even Frenchmen. Who knows though ? Maybe it'll do us good. Perhaps defeat will bring even Bishops to their senses. After all Huysmans touched bottom and bounced back."

"Defeat." The Archbishop was so shocked that he stood stock still for a moment. "But, Monsieur l'Abbé, there's that Maginot Line you've got."

"Which doesn't extend to the sea, Your Grace, and our disobedience extends everywhere." Moving on again the Abbé seemed to lose his train of thought, for by the time they reached the next forget-me-not lamp he was quoting Bernanos: "'*Le prêtre médiocre est entre tous impénétrable.*' One of the most frightening phenomena of this time of trouble is the dreadful ordinariness of the elect."

"We can't all be Dupanloups and Lacordaires, Monsieur l'Abbé."

"No, Your Grace; but we can be Hitlers. We can ram the fear of God down the throats of the tepid. There are times when I almost regret the abolition of the stake. When all's said and done there's nothing like a bundle of lighted faggots under a disbelieving arse for inculcating piety in the beholders."

"I think you're wrong," the Archbishop said when he had finished laughing. "Newman once said you couldn't argue men into belief, let alone torture them into it."

"Newman had never been to the *Folies Bergère*, Your Grace: therefore he couldn't understand French metaphysics. Not only does our belief not influence our conduct, but we allow our conduct to influence our belief. The Parisian industrialist who celebrates the descent of the Holy Ghost upon the Apostles by taking his typist to Deauville thinks that he has forfeited the *right* to believe in either the Holy Ghost or the Apostles. Arguing's no good with fools like that; the only solution's the thumbscrew."

" I've no doubt there are quite a few faulty syllogisms constructed at Brighton if it comes to the bit."

" It's not the same thing at all, Your Grace: Englishmen don't hate when they disbelieve; Frenchmen do. And the sneer, as Claudel says, has always been the mark of the damned, from Voltaire to Anatole France." The Archbishop didn't need the light from the pale blue lamps to see the unhappiness on the Abbé's lonely face. " I'm Curé now of a church near the Halles. Last year I had more than a hundred children making their first communion and swearing that they'd die rather than deny the Presence of Our Lord in the Blessed Sacrament. And how many of them do you think are still coming to Mass? Fifteen. Of course it's better than being Curé of St. Pierre de Chaillot or St. Honoré d'Eylau, and having all those selfish faces to be polite to at fashionable weddings. Don't you understand, Your Grace? I want to do a proper job of work. A priest's supposed to be the intermediary between God and man and in France the people have simply backed out. Whatever there's to be said for receiving baptism in

a state of unconsciousness it's scarcely to be recommended for Extreme Unction, and in most cases
we're lucky if we got as far as that."

The Abbé's anguish made the Archbishop realise
all over again how wrong he had been to be rude to
the Episcopal Dean in the tram four years ago. He
had always been grateful to Protestants for keeping
Catholics on their toes, and now he saw that he owed
them another debt: their incapacity for hatred of
God. Was this because the obedience asked of them
had not been so drastic? Would Frenchmen have been
better Christians if they'd had a complaisant Church
of France to be in subjective good faith about?

" The *Ville Lumière* was almost as bad as the *Ville
Blumière*," the Abbé Bonpapa said when they came
in sight of the towers of the cathedral black with age
like the river in the darkness. " And that goes for
the *inside* of churches too. ' The difference between an
electric bulb and a candle flame is the same as that
between a glass eye and a real one,' old Boni de
Castellane said. What a pity nobody ever thought of
making him Curé of the Madeleine!"

2

But the tapers round the bier in Notre Dame next
day were of real unbleached wax. The Archbishop of
Inchkeith and the Pentlands gave his absolution after
the Cardinal Bishop of Lille and prayed that God

might not enter into judgment with His Servant Jean, but would succour him with favour. M. Armand Lucot was among the bored-looking lay notabilities, and the Abbé Bonpapa reintroduced him to the Archbishop in the sacristy afterwards.

" When are you British going to send us some more soldiers?" the politician asked. "As a member of the French Cabinet I feel I've a right to know."

"As a Catholic prelate in a Protestant country I am not in my Government's secrets," the Archbishop answered and was glad that he wasn't: at the Lord Mayor's Banquet in 1939 Lord Halifax had pointed out that the British pact to help Poland had named no aggressor, and yet war had been declared only against Germany and not against Russia. The Pope's secrets must be complicated too: while a war of defence was justifiable, defence often meant attack, and attack meant sending boys of nineteen to murder other boys of nineteen, who had done them no harm and who in turn would be defending. Had Captain Inches been right in 1917 after all?

" As usual the British want to fight the war with French chests," M. Lucot said. " Sending us a hundred and ninety thousand men is a drop in the bucket compared with calling up five million."

" Most of the five million he talks about are still wearing their civilian shirts under their uniforms," the Abbé Bonpapa told the Archbishop when the politician had gone.

M. Théophraste however had bought himself an officer's khaki shirt and tie, and an officer's uniform too, with only a lance-corporal's silver stripe slanting on the sleeve to show that he was not a general. He was marching up and down between the tables, clicking his spurs against his leather leggings as he greeted customers, when the Archbishop and the Abbé arrived at his restaurant.

"He's guarding a boot factory at Clichy," the Abbé explained, "but as feeding *embusqués* is considered an essential part of the war effort, the boots are generally left in charge of the laces."

Lunch with hors d'œuvre, eggs or fish or meat, dessert and wine now cost thirty francs, the Archbishop saw; with hors d'œuvre, eggs or fish, meat, dessert and wine, thirty-five francs; with hors d'œuvre, eggs, fish, meat, dessert and wine, forty francs.

"Mauriac says that deep down within him every Frenchman knows that the religion he isn't practising is the true one," the Abbé said.

But the Archbishop wasn't listening: he was wondering whether, in recognition of the plenitude of his priesthood, the Vicar Capitulator had authorised the Abbé Bonpapa to offer him the whole shooting match this time.

CHAPTER XVI

IN THE second world war the Archbishop took his turn in the confessional, as the Old Jock had done in the first; but such a grand name on the box scared off a good many penitents, who preferred to be bawled out by Father O'Leary next door.

" So he gave you julery, did he? What was it now? A wrist watch or a bangle? "

Father O'Leary's shouting made it almost impossible for the Archbishop to hear what the pair of red tabs was telling him about the dance hostess at the Moulin Tartan. But with Generals announcing on the wireless how much they loved every man who killed a Nazi or a Fascist, the Archbishop thought that it must be hard for soldiers to practise purity and he let Red Tabs off with one of the Vicar-General's favourite quotations from Kierkegaard:

" ' If heaven loves one sinner more than ninety-nine just persons, the sinner does not know this from the beginning; on the contrary he is sensible only of heaven's wrath, until at last he, as it were, compels heaven to speak out.' "

" And if you don't promise to give back that bauble and never mind what your auntie says I'll have for to refuse you absolution "

How could the Holy Ghost be inspiring both his counsel and Father O'Leary's, the Archbishop wondered. Or had Divine Providence directed the footsteps of each penitent?

Divine Providence or not, the Archbishop had to leave the six or seven still waiting outside his box to Father O'Leary, so as to arrive in time with the Vicar-General at the Scottish Command chaplains' party at the Ossian Hotel. If they could not pray with their separated brethren, they could at least drink with them, Monsignor Samson-Slingsby had pointed out, and this was an excellent opportunity of showing that orthodoxy could on occasion produce as well-bred clergymen as heresy and schism.

" And what's more the Senior C. of E. bloke tells me they've organised cigars," the Vicar-General said, as they walked up the rubber-matted steps of the hotel.

But even cigar smoke could not prevent the Archbishop from seeing that the Vicar-General and himself wore the only black coats in a room packed with Sam Brownes and manly voices:

" Of course I told Ack and Quack to hell with their pull throughs I must have hymn books."

" I had to leave Elsie with her mother. Between you and me it's a bit of a bind this no love life business."

" Ebor nearly blew his top when I told him, and old Cantuar said that he was goddam well not going to stand for being bloody well bounced like that."

" What price infallibility now, Your Grace ? " It was the Episcopal Dean of course, in the uniform of a full Colonel. " Do you think that Britain would still rule the waves if the Pope ruled her ? "

Remembering how sorry he had been the last time he had lost his temper with Silly Ass Pearson, the Archbishop didn't even quote what Father O'Leary had said from the pulpit only last Sunday:

" If the nation hasn't got the grace of God in its heart, the biggest navy in the world will be no more use to it than a lot of wee paper boats floating down a gutter."

But the Archbishop was still feeling angry when he arrived at the new Free French Hostel to bless it, and he gave the volumes of Zola an extra whisk of holy water.

CHAPTER XVII

IF THE Vicar-General had introduced the Archbishop to Kierkegaard, the Abbé Bonpapa had put him on to Bernanos, and on his flight across to visit the French battlefields in 1944 the Archbishop opened *Journal d'un Curé de Campagne* and read:

" A poor lad who puts his girl in the family way one spring night, is considered by you to be in mortal sin, but the killer of a whole town, whilst the kids he's just poisoned'll be vomiting up their lungs on their mothers' laps, need only go off and change pants to ' distribute holy bread.' "

Wasn't that precisely what was happening in England at that very moment? Air Force chaplains shriving toughs of their fornications before they went to set fire to babies with phosphorus bombs? And the Catholic Hierarchy, himself included, hadn't said a word. Only the Anglican Dr. Bell of Chichester had seemed to understand that it was as cowardly to fire on women and children vertically as horizontally, and George Bernard Shaw that the torturer who didn't behold his victim's agony was as criminal as the one who did. The Abbé Bonpapa had been wrong; it wasn't a Hitler that the Church of God required; it was a Monty on the Papal throne, slinging Bishops out on their ears as though they were brigadiers.

" The General apologises for not having been able to come himself, sir, but he's got rather a lot on his plate just now," the Lieutenant-Colonel sent to meet the Archbishop at the airfield said. " The Germans are giving us a bit of stick. Nothing to worry about of course. There's no future in this war for the Hun."

The Archbishop tried to talk the language again:

" He's na poo, you mean."

" He's had it." ·

After searching the stupid face in vain for a sign of sorrow at the new rent in Christ's Garment, the Archbishop gave it up and sat in silence in the back of the staff car. Thirty million German communions had been made last year, he had read in the *Catholic Trumpet*, thirty million attempts at correspondence with grace. And thirty million failures probably. Even monks and nuns couldn't be in ignorance of what went on in Gestapo concentration camps. And some of those thirty million communicants had probably helped to flatten Coventry and let off V1's and V2's. It wasn't only the Hierarchies of Scotland and of England and Wales that had turned blind eyes and deaf ears: the German one was in it up to the neck too.

" A jeep was originally a G.P. which stood for ' General Purposes,' " the Lieutenant-Colonel was explaining as he showed the Archbishop into his room at the *château*. " I say, somebody's going to have a strip torn off them. I distinctly gave orders for the removal of Betty Grable."

" And who may she be ? " the Archbishop asked, smiling tolerantly at the pin-up.

" A film star, Your Grace. You know, like Veronica Lake. That's the form. Anyway I hope you don't think she's showing too much of the jolly old bosom."

" I think I'll survive," the Archbishop said. After all it was the busts that God had made, and the bombs that He hadn't.

" Goodee, Your Grace. I've always heard that you R.C.'s were much more broadminded than our washouts."

" I assure you, Colonel, it doesn't go for everything. We can dig our toes in pretty firmly when we like."

" Smithley-Craven's been telling me what a good scout Your Grace is," the General said when he greeted the Archbishop in the ante-room and introduced him to his Brigadier and a ring of friendly looking full Colonels.

" That's what I like about you fellows," the Brigadier said when they sat down at table. " You can put it away like Admirals."

In 1916, the Archbishop remembered, it had been like a fish.

" Let's say like a petty officer." Anxious not to let the side down from motives of human respect, the Archbishop added: " It's only *excess* in pleasure that the Church condemns."

" That goes for the women too, doesn't it, Your Grace ? " a Colonel asked. " I remember an R.C. padre we once had in Peshawar. Anyway what he did with the hospital nurses after dark was nobody's business. Of course when he was on parade he was on parade."

" I think, Colonel, that you must have been mistaken."

But they were all laughing so loudly that nobody heard.

" That's what I like about your show, Your Grace," the General said. " There's no arguing. An order's an order. You stuff them full of the jolly old tommy rot and Bob's your uncle."

" Come clean now, Your Grace," the Brigadier said. " How much of it do you really believe yourself? Strictly off the record of course."

The Archbishop was appalled. So this was what supposedly intelligent Protestants really thought about the Church: that its priests were lechers who deliberately taught error to the uneducated. Even Arnold Bennett, he remembered, had described an ordination he had witnessed in St. Sulpice in 1910 as " a startling mummery."

" To begin with," he said in an unsteady voice, " priests do not have mistresses. Those who have them on the sly and are found out are suspended *a divinis*. To end with, every bishop and priest in the Catholic Church is implicitly convinced of the truth of the doctrines he teaches."

The General was the first to break the unhappy silence.

" I'm sorry, Your Grace, if we've made a nonsense of it," he said. " And I'm sure Harkness is too. Aren't you, Harkness? "

" Of course," the Brigadier said at once.

" Bing Crosby's an R.C. too, isn't he, Your Grace?"

Afraid that he had rebuked ignorance instead of removing it, the Archbishop went on more gently:

" You see, what the Church teaches is not as silly as you think. We don't know enough about the world to understand what makes sense in God's eyes and what doesn't. It's like a cat having canker powder put in its ears: the cat doesn't understand the purpose but it thinks it understands the sting." Then he remembered Newman's remark about the folly of attempting to argue men into belief and said: " Anyway, the Admiral thinks he would like another spot, General, if you don't mind."

But they had all spoken their minds too freely for even port to make them recover their jollity, and the Archbishop had to try not to notice how relieved they were when he asked to be allowed to retire. When he got to his bedroom he found that the pin-up had been replaced by " Behold, I stand and knock," and was now humble enough not to be sorry; after all, Holman Hunt was probably better for Archbishops than Betty Lake or Veronica Gable or whatever her name had been.

2

Most of the Italians in the prisoner-of-war camp at Inverbuchanty, the Archbishop knew, only came to Mass on Sunday because Mass came to them, and for this reason he went out to examine adult candidates for confirmation personally as soon as he had returned from his visit to the front.

" How many Persons are there in the Blessed Trinity, Giuseppe ? " he asked one of them.

" Three, Your Excellency: the Father, the Son and St. Anthony of Padua."

By what stretch of imagination could this be interpreted as implicit faith, the Archbishop wondered. Then he remembered his sermon to the Catholics in the 51st Division. " Be faithful to that girl at home who's eating out her heart for you," he had told the pie faces that might not after all have had pie souls; not a word about the thuggery that was now as organised on one side as on the other. It was the Archbishop of Inchkeith and the Pentlands that His Holiness Pope Monty I ought to be slinging out on his ear. How could the laity be expected to understand theology when there was so much scrubbing at the clergy to be done first ?

" The Father, the Son, and *the Holy Ghost*," the Archbishop said gently. " All right, Giuseppe; I'll confirm you."

CHAPTER XVIII

ROME HOWEVER seemed to think more highly of His Grace than His Grace of himself, for in January 1946 " Our Most Loyal Son the Lord Archbishop of Inchkeith and Pentlands " was raised to the Sacred Purple. Among the thirty other Cardinals created were Monsignor Pantachini, the Bishop of Minnehaha, the Bishops of Bovisa and Spartivento, and Monsignor Wumerumbani, for kerygmatic catechesis.

Waiting in the ante-camera for his private audience with the Pope, the Archbishop of Inchkeith and the Pentlands met a tall cold Cardinal coming out, and from the beauty of his face recognised the Archbishop of Milan whose hands had entranced Christendom when he had sung one of the nine pontifical requiem Masses during the Novendial for Pius XI.

" Inchkeith and the Pentlands, Your Eminence," the Archbishop said in answer to the Cardinal's look of enquiry. " Scotland," he added, knowing that geography wasn't one of the subjects about which the Holy Ghost enlightened Italian prelates. " And the first Scottish Cardinal to be created since Cardinal Beaton, Archbishop of St. Andrews, Bishop of Mirepoix and Lord Abbot of Arbroath was assassinated in 1545."

" Ah, Scotland Yard, the great detective." The Cardinal Archbishop of Milan, Cardinal Priest of the church of Saints Sylvester and Martin, formerly Lord Abbott of St. Paul's-without-the-Walls, bowed and walked on.

Like Pius XI, Pius XII rose from his desk to greet the Archbishop and to bless him. The war had interrupted the Archbishop's visits *ad limina*, and it was the first time the Archbishop had seen the new Pope. Behind the thick spectacles, the gentle eyes looked tired. " I mount not upon a throne, but upon a crucifix," Eugenio Pacelli had said at his election in 1939, as though foreseeing the Church of Silence over which he was so shortly to reign.

" Now tell me about," the Pope said as he led the Archbishop up to the desk.

" Oh, we're getting on, Your Holiness, but not as well as we ought to. The Presbyterians are still hostile and neither I nor my colleagues are invited to official functions."

" But to Cowes you are invited, yes ? "

" Cowes is in England, Your Holiness."

" And Archbishop Griffin ? He is invited, no ? "

" There haven't been any regattas since the war, Your Holiness."

" But now that the war is done and over with Archbishop Griffin will be invited to Cowes, no ? "

" I don't think so, Your Holiness. Indeed I don't even think the Archbishop of Canterbury is."

" Then it is a pity. It used to be such a good race. And how angry in 1893 was your Edward King when the *Meteor* of Kaiser Wilhelm beat the *Britannia* of him."

Was this what Pius IX and Leo XIII had hobnobbed about with Manning? Was this what had nearly lost Newman his Red Hat? Was it the Solent that was keeping Ronnie Knox out? Was this why Popes had always been so notoriously ill-informed about the Church in England?

" On the whole it is perhaps just as well that the Catholic Hierarchy in Britain is not invited to take part in these festivities," the Archbishop said. " In that way it's easier for us to render unto Cæsar without worshipping Mammon."

" And in 1896 your Edward King was more angrier still when the second *Meteor* of the Kaiser beat another *Britannia* of him."

" *Neque enim Petri successoribus Spiritus Sanctus promissus est, ut eo revelante novam doctrinam pate- facerent . . .*" If the Father of Christendom kept on talking about yachting to the first Scottish Cardinal since Beaton it could mean only that His Holiness was trying to assess his new Eminence's other-worldliness.

" We've always had to fight for our religion in Scotland, Your Holiness," the Archbishop said. " We've been too busy being ridiculed and bearing witness to have had any time, let alone any inclination, for gallivanting."

" It was at Cowes in 1887 that your great Churchill first meeted your King George the Fifth."

Did the Pope only *speak*, but not understand, English, the Archbishop wondered. Or was His Holiness trying to snub him? One never knew where one was with Italians, even when they were Popes. If the Archbishop had ever to attend a conclave he would vote for His Eminence Finbar Cardinal Magillycuddy-Tuohy, Lord Bishop of Minnehaha: the Holy Ghost would have to work overtime if either His Eminence Wearie Willie or His Eminence Tired Tim got in.

" Make unto yourself friends of the mammon of unrighteousness, my son," the Pope said as he pressed the bell on his desk.

2

The brief of appointment was handed to the Archbishop in the Scots College in the via Quattro Fontane by two papal couriers; and among those who came to congratulate the new Cardinal at the *visita di calore* was the Abbé Bonpapa.

" You see, Eminence, how right I was about France touching bottom like Huysmans. We're bouncing back now. The Occupation's woken us up. Do you know what I'm here about? Worker priests. The Curé d'Ars wanted a priest in every parish. Soon we're going to have one in every factory. French

Christians are going to get down to it at last. And high time too. The Eldest Daughter of the Church has been kicking up her heels for long enough."

" Like Mistinguett," the Cardinal said.

" All the same I'd rather sit next her in heaven than Savonarola," the Abbé said as he made way for a group of Ceylonese seminarists.

" Wish I could put on dog the way old Spelly does," the Cardinal Bishop of Minnehaha said when he went with Cardinal Campbell to the Sistine Chapel next day, to robe in the *cappa magna* for the first time. " Innitzer's the boy for me though. Travelled up third class from Vienna without any socks on and then gets in Dutch with the Secretary of State for going around the Vatican and switching off all the unnecessary lights."

The procession to the Hall of Benedictions was led by the Cardinal Patriarch of Armenia. Behind the Archbishop of Westminster came the Archbishop of Inchkeith and the Pentlands, with a Privy Chamberlain of the Sword and Cape on his right, and Monsignor Brodie, his private secretary, on his left.

Seated on one of the thirty red damask chairs drawn up in a semi-circle round the throne, Cardinal Campbell thought that the Pope's sad eyes were fixed more often on him than on any of the others. Had he gone too far with his remark about " gallivanting " ? The way the scarlet biretta was almost banged on his head suggested that he had, and the Pope's allocution about the terrible responsibilities carried by Cardinals in an upset, post-war world seemed to be directed particularly at himself.

3

His uneasiness was still with him next day when he knelt with his twenty-nine brethren in the Blessed Sacrament chapel of St. Peter's and swore that he would always defend the rights of Holy Mother Church. He was frightened by the cold clever faces of the old Cardinals who came to lead the new Cardinals to the papal throne erected above the tomb of the Apostle. And when his turn came to go forward and kneel before the Pope it seemed that even kerygmatic catechesis had been more loudly applauded. ". . . *accipe galerum rubrum* . . ." ". . . receive the red hat . . ." the Pope said to Cardinal Campbell and smiled as he added in English: " Bonny Scotland!"

4

Miss Assisi was getting old too now and he looked more like Donald Duck than a pin up Cardinal when he took Cardinal Campbell to dine in a restaurant off the via Veneto.

" *Cosa vuol prendere, Eminentissimo?* " he asked as he handed Cardinal Campbell the menu card.

" *Osso buco, Eminentissimo*, I think," Cardinal Campbell said and handed back the card.

" Spaghetti for me, Eminentissimo," the Cardinal Priest of Santa Rita fuori-la-Città said as he held out the card with his thumbnail under the price of *osso buco* so that the Cardinal Priest of San Babila-sulla-via-Appia could see that it cost six hundred lire as against three hundred for spaghetti. Despite the Diocese of Minnehaha, it was clear that Peter's Pence had not yet become Peter's Dough.

" On second thoughts, Eminentissimo, I'll have spaghetti too," Cardinal Campbell said.

" That's right, Eminentissimo. When in Rome do as the Romans."

" I say, Crystal," a British officer said loudly to the A.T.S. he was dining with, " those two old cocks over there are Cardinals."

" So might you be, Buster, if you couldn't help it."

" Democracy," Cardinal Campbell said in case Miss Assisi had overheard too.

" Democracy, Eminentissimo, is like giving a box of matches and a stick of dynamite to a child: sooner or later you know he's going to blow himself up. Elections ought to be like marriage: voters ought to be forced to go to confession first."

" Really to be a Christian, Eminentissimo, one must be free not to be a Christian."

" You are wrong, Eminentissimo: really to be a Christian one must be *taught* to be a Christian."

" I agree, Eminentissimo—provided the person who is taught to be a Christian is also free not to be a Christian afterwards."

The Italian Cardinal smiled pityingly.

" You Anglo-Saxons are all the same," he said. " You see world problems in terms of the conditions obtaining in your own countries. You forget that the Church is Universal and has to deal with nations who do not see morality in terms of sport. Latin Christians, even when properly instructed, have got to be *compelled* to virtue. And it doesn't stop there either, Eminentissimo. Whatever the crimes of a particular Government may be the Church must come to terms with it so that the Christians living under its rule can go to the Sacraments, receive grace and save their souls. The means may not be used, of course, but the means must be there."

" Perhaps I'll surprise you by going even further than that, Eminentissimo: if the world's not going to sink back into savagery the means must not only be there; they must be used. Now all those Bishops we saw in St. Peter's this morning, in their organised tiers of inefficiency, what are they going to do about it?"

" Almost certainly what they've always done about it, Eminentissimo: nothing. However neither their laziness not their platitudes can alter the fact that they and they alone are the link with the first Pentecost."

" But surely even a *link* with the first Pentecost ought to speak out, Eminentissimo. And it's speaking out that's wanted, speaking out from the right people about the things that are wrong, definite damnings of definite deeds. Umbrella condemnations of governmental iniquities are no good. We're only a minority in the Archdiocese of Inchkeith and the Pentlands, but we're braver than that."

" Has Your Eminence never heard the story of the Frenchwoman who complained to her confessor about the slovenliness and lethargy of the Roman clergy? ' *Madame,*' the confessor said, ' *je vous ai toujours dit qu'il ne fallait pas visiter la cuisine du Bon Dieu.*' "

" I'd soon put a little order in God's kitchen if I were Pope," Cardinal Campbell said.

"You never will be, Eminentissimo. Not unless you learn to eat spaghetti more neatly than that. A twirl and then a swing, Eminentissimo. Like the celebrant with the thurible in the Ambrosian Rite. Look." Miss Assisi's fork wound up a hank of spaghetti as effortlessly as a windlass. " It's quite simple really."

Cardinal Campbell gave up arguing.

" Cigarette, Eminentissimo ? " he said as he held out his cigarette case when the coffee came.

" Lucky Strike, Eminentissimo? They're my favourites," Miss Assisi said as he helped himself to five. " Black market, I presume ? "

" No, Eminentissimo. Red Cardinal. Of Minnehaha to be precise."

" He never gave *me* any, the dirty dog. And I let
him into the Holy Father before Spellman too.
Anyway there's one who'll never be Pope."

" Minnehaha, Eminentissimo? I don't suppose for
one moment he wants to be."

" No, Eminentissimo; Spellman."

" Why, Eminentissimo? Don't tell me *he* can't eat
spaghetti properly."

But Miss Assisi refused to be drawn.

5

Protestants as well as Catholics turned out to greet
the new Cardinal when he arrived home. The
charwomen, labourers, sailors and prostitutes who had
lined the streets for the Old Jock's funeral lined them
again for him and waved and cheered. The Cardinal
blessed them all, trying to warm each loneliness behind
the jubilation. The Thistle Hotel, he saw with
amusement, had run up the Papal flag. If he wasn't
making unto himself friends of the mammon of
unrighteousness, the mammon of unrighteousness
seemed to be holding out a hand to him.

CHAPTER XIX

THE PATTERN, the Cardinal thought, as he sat reading The *Pentlands Evening Pibroch* in 1952, was very much what it had been after the previous war: Royalty was walking round paddocks; statesmen were talking about a Just and Lasting Peace; in Tuckahoe (Virginia) a stamp machine had been invented which said " Thank You " when a coin was inserted in the slot; and the wife of a Baptist clergy-man in the West Riding of Yorkshire Thought Sex Should Be Taught at Five.

After which it was almost a relief to have to preside at the lecture on Existentialism which the Vicar-General was giving to the Guild of Our Lady of Perpetual Succour in the cathedral hall. The atten-dance, the Cardinal was not surprised to see, was meagre, and most of the applause for his own red sash and skull cap.

" There are two kinds of existentialism: Christian and pagan," the Vicar-General began to read from a wodge of typescript as thick as a foundation stone. " Of the latter Jean-Paul Sartre, who blasphemously asserts that he has ' suppressed God the Father,' is the chief exponent. The essence of a pencil, Sartre

says, precedes its existence, because prior to its manu-
facture its qualities have been conceived in the mind
of its inventor; whereas the existence of man, he states,
precedes man's essence, which man himself creates by
the choice of conduct he makes after he has begun to
exist."

The drone, which during the war had never failed
to send the Polish Brigade to sleep on the Commemoration of the Finding of the Holy Cross, quickly
had the Guild of Our Lady of Perpetual Succour
nodding, and it was only by setting himself to criticise
that the Cardinal kept his thoughts from wandering.
Was this sort of thing really what the doctor ordered?
Was this giving a reason for not reasoning? Was this
the way to stop the clever young men from taking the
part for the whole and denying that the whole could
even be a part? Was this the answer that Father
Martindale had expected when he had written that
the world had become too horrible for those who
professed to examine its problems to remain on
polite surfaces?

" ' Existence appears, can be encountered, but
never inferred,' Sartre makes Roquentin say in *La
Nausée*. This, dear members of the Guild of Our
Lady of Perpetual Succour, is an argument which it
is extremely difficult for us to answer."

Poor Vicar-General, the Cardinal thought: Mrs.
Flaherty and Mrs. O'Toole would answer Jean-Paul
Sartre as they had answered George Bernard Shaw,

H. G. Wells and Immanuel Kant: by the simple process of not reading him.

" ' *Cette ignoble marmelade*,' Roquentin called all living creation as revelation came to him in the public park at Bouville."

Roquentin was right, the Cardinal told himself. One thing was certain: the existence of the ignoble marmalade had to precede the essence of TV or the Light Programme. One of the proofs of Christ's Divinity was that He had never talked like a Labour M.P. Apart from revelation, it was hard not to think that the world would not have been a happier place to dwell in if 99% of the ignoble marmalade had been washed down the drain. The Trinity was child's-play to understand compared with the number of by-products God seemed to require.

" What can we in the spatio-temporal world know of what Gabriel Marcel calls the Absolute Thou? Nothing, if we are to believe Kierkegaard. ' So also with the proof of God's existence,' he says. ' As long as I keep hold of the proof, that is, continue to demonstrate, the existence does not come out, if for no other reason than I am engaged in proving it; but when I let the proof go the existence is there.' "

Looking to see how far the Vicar-General's pile of typescript had diminished, the Cardinal saw with dismay that it was still the same height as before, and that it was impossible to measure the dose of metaphysics yet to come, because as he finished each page

198

the Monsignor was sliding it under those still to be read.

Kierkegaard was wrong, the Cardinal avenged himself by thinking. The proof was there for all to see. The proof was in the miracles wrought every year at Lourdes. The proof was in the priests with faces like stockbrokers. The proof was in the compulsion to pity. The world had a third choice all right between concentration camps and strip cartoons.

2

" That ought to have made 'em sit up and take notice, Eminence, don't you think? " the Vicar-General said as they walked back through the underground passage to the clergy house side by side in their silk coloured cloaks. " At least they'll no longer have any excuse for making the sort of stupid mistake as Aldous Huxley and saying that the ' thou ' is identical with the ' that.' "

Wasn't it? The Cardinal wanted to say that there were probably more readers of Annie S. Swan in heaven than of Huxley, and then remembered what the Old Jock had said at his ordination about St. Francis of Sales having been canonised for his politeness to bores. " Anyway I'm sure you've got it well into their heads that existence precedes essence."

" Eminence, you're killing me." Misery had drained the last touch of worldliness from the Vicar-

General's porty cheeks. "That's what *Sartre* says; it's not what *I* say. Who's going to understand if you don't?"

Who indeed, the Cardinal wondered.

"That book of yours, Monsignor," he said kindly. "It must be coming along now."

"That's just what I was going to speak to you about, Eminence. It's finished. Those were extracts from it I was reading tonight."

"Excellent news, Monsignor, excellent, really excellent," the Cardinal said, hoping that he looked as though he felt that it was. Forty-five years Monsignor Samson-Slingsby had slaved at those incomprehensibilities; it was a good thing the scholastic world was less limited than the Guild of Our Lady of Perpetual Succour and himself. "You're wanting a *Censor Deputatus*, that it? Well, what about Brodie?"

"Brodie! Brodie's no good. Why I doubt if he even knows the difference between *l'en soi* and *le pour soi*."

"To tell you the truth, Monsignor, I very much doubt if I do either."

"You're different, Eminence. You've got brains. You'll soon learn. It's as easy as falling off a log really. All that Your Eminence has got to bear in mind is that we've got to answer the atheistic existentialists in their own language if we are ever going to be able to get any authentic existence going at all. In other words the only way to answer falsely asserted fact is with real fact and not with emotion. Anyway I think you'll find my book as lucid as my lecture."

Touched by the plea in the quirky eyes, the Cardinal gave in.

" All right, Monsignor, I'll read it for you," he said. " And now if you'll come to my room I think I've got three more slivers of soap for you."

" Stickers, Your Eminence! " The Vicar-General followed the Cardinal upstairs so eagerly that he nearly knocked him over. " The main thing is to get hold of them before they break into little bits."

CHAPTER XX

WHEN THE Cardinal went to New York in 1954 he found that the Acropolis and Parthenon had come on in twenty years: although the basin in his bedroom was still blocked there was a plug on the end of the bath chain. After ringing in vain for somebody to remove the tumblers and empty bottles left behind by the previous occupant, the Cardinal went down to the Ace of Hearts Bar, " a peaceful backwater away from the rushing tides of the workaday world," where Monsignor Rooney had elected to wait for him in a corner of Turkish Delight gloom.

" Two whispers, king size," the Monsignor said to a waitress in transparent black nylon pantaloons.

" Before I forget, Eminence, the boys asked me to tell you how glad they are about your having made the grade. And what is Your Eminence panhandling for this time, may I ask? Shawls for unmarried mothers or mitres for unmarried bishops? "

" Same old thing, Monsignor, I'm afraid: still my cathedral sanctuary."

"Well, whatever you do, Eminence, don't let the nuns catch you popping to see a film called *The French Line* on the sly. Seems the way Jane Russell almost shows her can to the camera is nobody's business. Anyway the Archbishop of Saint Louis has made it a mortal sin for anybody in his diocese to see it."

" And napalm? " the Cardinal asked. " Are any of your Archbishops or Bishops doing anything about that? "

" You're getting your wires crossed, aren't you, Your Eminence? Napalm's the Pentagon's job." The Monsignor raised his glass. " Gin, vodka, vermouth, that's the mixture. Have a big time, Your Eminence. And I shouldn't worry my head too much about Jane Russell if I were you. She's got no point of view. She's just a big dish that comes on."

" That's what I'm trying to get at, Monsignor. Until we stop conniving at men killing other men by violence we'll always have big dishes that come on."

" That's the moot point, Your Eminence: which

came first, the dagger or the dish? Spelly thinks it was the dish."

" Cleopatra's nose, you mean?"

" Spelly doesn't think it was only her nose."

The Cardinal said no more. What right had he to criticise the Archbishop of St. Louis for speaking out about the dish when he himself had been so silent about the dagger?"

" All's well with the world," Monsignor Rooney said as he raised his second king size.

" Except that at this very moment eighteen thousand three hundred and fifty-seven tubercular children are breathing their last."

" What I say is it's a Christian's duty to look on the bright side of things, Your Eminence. Anyway the Church has got nothing to fear provided Cardinals and Archbishops and Bishops don't start bugging out on one another."

The Cardinal gave it up: perhaps the Holy Ghost was busy in South Dakota, bending the rigid, calming the turgid, warming the frigid.

" Now look here, Your Eminence, ordinarily I'd lose my best cassock rather than let a Britisher pick up a check, see? But, well, a mere Monsignor can't risk getting in Dutch with a Cardinal, can he?"

" You bet," the Cardinal said and took the cardboard bill from the dish held out to him by the dish.

2

The air hostess on the plane to Sioux Falls was a dish too, and seemed to know it, but the Cardinal was too busy reading a bound proof of *Freewill and the Molecule* to pay her much attention:

"In order fully to comprehend the empirical we must first of all condition ourselves to understand the potential which may be described as the mystical which in turn may be described as the radiation of consciousness towards Being."

"Micky Spillane, Reverend?" the fat man sitting next the Cardinal asked.

"I wish it were." The Cardinal half-closed the proof, keeping his thumb in to mark his place. "Just the philosophy of religion, I'm afraid."

"Well, what do you know? I'm a religious man myself, Reverend. Or I guess I would be if it weren't for this no booze and no dames business. And then the way the Churches differ among themselves just burns me up. The Baptists give you one *spiel* and the Congregationalists another and the Catholic yarn don't stack up with the Presbyterian one. So what's a poor guy like me to do, Reverend? That's what I want to know."

"Just stick to the no booze and the no dames, I suppose," the Cardinal said, thankful that his overcoat concealed the red silk under his collar.

"That's a holy God miss, Reverend, if ever there was one. What guys like me want to do is to have all the booze and the dames we can lay our hands on and then the Churches will be forced to do a grand get-together to make us keep off the booze and the dames, see?"

"Well, that's certainly an angle," the Cardinal said.

"Oh, I'm a great one when it comes to finding angles. There's that wife of mine, see? 'Now look here, Sue,' I says to her, 'what about us putting that dough we've saved in the Union Dime?' 'No, Joe,' she says—my name's Joseph, see? but Susan always calls me Joe like I always call her Sue, see?— 'No, Joe,' she says, 'we'll go out and get us a good time.' Dime time, poetry, see? But I wasn't to be had that way. 'Now, look here, Sue,' I says, 'all this sleeping in the raw your Ma's always raving about, well it's kind of rugged when a man's own wife starts using her sex on him like a hoodlum uses a gun.' She didn't take a rain check for that one, see?"

The Cardinal thought that even Monsignor Samson-Spillane might sound a little simpler:

"To the cogitational *ego* of Descartes must be added the notional *moi* of Sartre."

"That's right, Reverend, have a bit of shut eye," the fat man said. "I'll watch that cutie of a hostess for Mrs. Reverend."

" She'll be grateful, I'm sure," the Cardinal murmured drowsily.

3

At the reception in the Tomahawk Hotel the Cardinal Archbishop of Inchkeith and the Pentlands and the Cardinal Bishop of Minnehaha stood side by side to greet the guests announced by the liveried butler:

" Mrs. J. Carruthers Stubgutt."

" Cousin by marriage of Mrs. B. Merchiston Stubgutt," the Cardinal Bishop said out of the side of his mouth. " Both of 'em set straight for hell fire."

" Father Aloysius MacDonald, Father Humbert Stein, Father Shamus McManus."

" Knuckleheads, all three of 'em."

" Miss Moira Rattigan."

" Regular First Friday-er but inclined on occasion to throw her bikini over the pastoral."

" Mr. Aelred Saint Aubin Colquhoun."

" Editor of the *Minnehaha Catholic Argus*. A proper hoss's ass if ever there were one. Hya, Aelred? Meet the Cardinal Archbishop of Inchkeith and the Pentlands. I've just been telling His Nibs about those deep-oh leading articles of yours."

" Father John Henry Newman Casabianca. Father Casal de Buison O'Grady. Father Spike Karczmarzyck, Father Ludovic van Schoonenberg." The

Holy Church throughout the world shook hands with both Cardinals and rushed off to confess the Father of Incomprehensible Majesty behind double highballs.

"Now, Eminence, you'd better do some mixing," the Cardinal Bishop of Minnehaha said. "And when Your Eminence has had enough just pinch my battam and we'll beat it."

"Funnily enough, Your Eminence, I'm going to Scotland for my vacation this year," Miss Moira Rattigan said. "Now where does Your Eminence think I'm likely to find the very smallest piece of tartan there is in existence?"

"Mr. Carruthers Stubgutt said she'd said there were aborigines in Austria but I said to Mr. Carruthers Stubgutt that of course she'd meant Australia. I was right, Your Eminence, don't you think?"

"The answer, Your Eminence, isn't liturgy in the common tongue but music in the common chant like the Indian epics and puranas Rāmāyana and Mahābharata."

"Has Your Eminence read the Life of St. Quitteria of Portugal? She was a hot rod if ever there was one."

"A hot rod for God, Father Spike means, of course, Your Eminence."

"What does Your Eminence think of the new Dutch methodology? The *Samengesteld door het Katechetisch Centrum Canisianum en de Katechetische Werkgroep van de Broeders van de Onbevlekte Ontvan-*

genis te Maastricht boys seem to be the answer to a maiden's prayer, doesn't Your Eminence think?"

"Now, Your Eminence, don't try to get out of things. Your Eminence hasn't told me yet where I'm likely to find the smallest piece of tartan in existence."

"In Basle," the Cardinal said as he reached out for his brother Cardinal's passing sash.

4

"*Ubi Sheen, ibi Ecclesia*," Sister Scholastica said as she switched off the handsome Bishop on the gas station parlour television screen and turned on the wireless instead.

"Our best wishes to the Camp Fire girls of Watertown for their birthday week," the wireless said. "Nothing adds so much to the dignity of summer living as a lovely garden. You can get a complete garden for twenty bucks down."

"Would you believe it, Your Eminence?" Sister Scholastica said to Cardinal Campbell. "The non-sense the agnostics can talk! 'Is God a Conditioned Reflex?' was the title of an article I read the other day."

"It's worse than that, Lou," the Cardinal Bishop of Minnehaha said. "Those literary gleeps are killing charity. Soon a guy won't be able to get a good review unless he writes 'Women and Children Last.'"

"Purple's a colour of shadows and far away hills,

more asthmatic than climatic," the wireless said.
" Do you know, folks, I'd say there was something
mighty blue about purple ? "

" The literature of the thirties consisted in the
telling of bad deeds in good prose and that of the
fifties of worse deeds in better prose," Cardinal
Campbell said.

" Ladies, I'd like to try a sound any housekeeper
knows—the sound of money," the wireless said. " Get
a package of new blue detergent soap suds."

" That's no excuse for *us*, Your Eminence," Sister
Scholastica said. " After all the Church of God knew
about hot pants long before Tennessee Williams."

" And now for the story of Sally and Mike," the
wireless said. " Mike was standing there at the edge
of the swimming pool with an Ephraim Rustless
Special on his wrist and Sally said to him ' Ten bucks
if you dive in with your clothes on,' so of course
Mike dove."

" Graham Greene seems to have an inkling though,
Lou, don't you think ? " the Cardinal Bishop of
Minnehaha said.

" Oh, I grant you, Finbar, we're *coming along*,"
Sister Scholastica said.

" The finest form of evaporated milk brings a
recipe for a hearty meal and a failure-proof creamy
sauce," the wireless said.

" But Dorothy Day's the only Catholic writer that's
likely to go straight to heaven," Sister Scholastica

said. " Remind me, Eminence, before you go away to give you a copy of Reverend Mother's latest: *The Life of St. Quitteria of Portugal.*"

" I'm honoured, I'm sure," Cardinal Campbell said.

" Don't be: it's screwball," Sister Scholastica said.

" Well, Bernie, we made that record together, didn't we ? " the wireless said.

5

Packing next morning in his bedroom, Cardinal Campbell found that he had room in his suitcase either for his shirts just back from the laundry, or for the *Life of St. Quitteria of Portugal* by Reverend Mother Bibiana Chrysostom Murphy, *Soaring Souls* by Rev. R. Baerlein O.F.M., and *Serving God in Paris (Ill.)* by a sister of the Immaculate Heart of Mary; the shirts won.

CHAPTER XXI

By ALL SOULS' DAY 1955 the Vicars Apostolic on the walls of the Cardinal's study were beginning to look less misty and even the Old Jock himself young, but the Cardinal still sang his third Mass for the dead in the presence of the cathedral chapter. He prayed for the unfaithful departed as well as for the faithful, for George Bernard Shaw as well as for Francis Cardinal Bourne, for the living as well as for the dead, for President Eisenhower, Diana Dors, the authoress of I GAVE SAMBO A DRINK OF HOLY WATER in the *Catholic Trumpet*, and the Redemptorist Missioner who had said that expecting the average Christian to correspond with grace was like waiting for Gina Lollobrigida outside the back door of the Scratcher.

"Cheery-ta-ta, Your Eminence, be good," a woman he did not know shouted to the Cardinal that evening as he came out of the cathedral clergy house on his way to the Artists' Institute dinner.

Decidedly, the Cardinal thought as he smiled and waved back, it was getting less cauld up on top. Even Protestants were impressed by the red sock he now wore on the left foot he kicked with. By living all his life in this town he seemed to have made it more of a real place than Rome, Paris, San Firmín de las Estrellas, Sioux Falls or any of the towns he had known only fleetingly, and he sometimes found it difficult to think that these were just as real.

"Mind yer heid now, Yer Eminence," the chauffeur-gardener-sacristan said as the Cardinal bent to get into the Morris Minor which the Archdiocese was able to afford again now there was enough money in the Union Bank of Scotland No. 2 Account for the completion of the new sanctuary.

"Bishops should not ought to be big men," Pius XI

had said. If he had been smaller would he have been invited to the Artists' Institute dinner long before this? As it was he was uneasy: painters these days were reputed to be as irreligious as the writers whose blasphemies spoiled his Sunday afternoons. The Cardinal thought again of Pius XI, shaking hands with Say Ten many times a day, and envied the composure of Royalty, able to smile at anything from an Ambassador to a cod-fish on a slab.

At first it was even worse than he had expected: the issue benevolence put on to smooth out rebellion in wrinkles, the arrogant women with stupidity stamped on their faces like a kick from a horse, it took the Cardinal all the discipline of forty years of priesthood to hide his knowledge that he had less in common with them than with St. Thomas of Aquin or with future bishops in unborn wombs; and the Episcopal Dean, pillared on his gaiters, didn't help with his crack:

" Why is it only when he's making a *statement* that His Holiness is infallible? Why not when he's praying? Why were his requests to God to stop the war no more granted than those of the Moderator of the General Assembly or the Archbishop of Canterbury?"

" Well the war *was* stopped in the end, wasn't it?" But the Cardinal knew that this was cheating and that the disbelieving snouts stuck into glasses round his red cloak required a better answer than that. " ' Knock

A Thread of Scarlet

and it shall be opened unto you,' I know Our Lord
said. But we are apt to forget that complete self-
abnegation is the mallet, and even Popes are not
always heroic enough to be able to use it. The Curé
d'Ars who starved himself and slept with a log for a
pillow—his prayers were always granted. And there's
another thing: we've got to ask for the right things.
Our Lord is scarcely likely to set the supernatural
machinery in motion just to provide a stockbroker
with a set of new tyres or a holiday at Juan-les-Pins."

"Thanks, Your Eminence, I'm a stockbroker," a
man with a nose like an end-of-season strawberry
said.

"On the whole I'm inclined to think that there's
something in what His Eminence has just been telling
us," the Minister of the Town Kirk said. "I once
met a Jesuit in Lyons who seemed to be genu-inely
concerned with the speeritual welfare of his peepul."

"All the same, Your Eminence, they say that some
of those women in those French houses—well, Your
Eminence, that they're a little bit fast," the stockbroker
said.

"They're closed now, Scrymegeour-Duncan," the
Episcopal Dean said.

"Nothing like the *Church Times* for keeping a
fellow up to date, is there?" the stockbroker said.

"The Festival now, Your Eminence," the President
said as he led the Cardinal into the dining-room.
"Why on earth it should always be held in Edinburgh

beats me. I don't know what Your Eminence thinks but seems to me that even Falkirk knows more about art than the quarter-educated *bourgeoisie* of Murrayfield. The *Dos de Mayo* in the Prado for example. How many bankers in Morningside have even heard of it?"

"Give me the *Tres de Mayo* any day of the week!" Even at table the Cardinal wasn't going to get away from Silly Ass Pearson, plumped down opposite and butting in again almost before the Cardinal had finished saying grace. "But El Greco's the boy! *El Entierro del Conde de Orgaz.* There's a picture for you! His Apostles now, Your Eminence? A little bit too existentialist perhaps?"

"I wonder, Dean. I don't quite see how one can trace the notional *moi* of Sartre on a canvas. And then El Greco would have had to daub *l'en soi* and *le pour soi* on top of that, wouldn't he? But who knows? Perhaps he was a prophet as well as painter."

Which, as the Cardinal had hoped, silenced the Dean for quite a bit; but with the brandy he came bobbing back:

"This Pope business, Your Eminence. You've never really answered my question, have you? At what precise moment does the old boy become infallible? Is it when he's elected? Or when the Dean of the Sacred College places the triple crown on his nut? Or is it at his ordination? Or when he's baptised?"

"When he learns to eat spaghetti properly."

After that the Cardinal could do what he liked with them all; but he punished himself for his unkindness to Silly Ass Pearson by not quoting the passage from Eric Gill which he had learned by heart to impress them:

"Many men quarrel with art, however good, because they are prudes. And this quarrel can never be settled until men of prudence are artists, and most artists are men of prudence."

"Still a good Kartholic, Your Eminence, I hope?" the flatfooted waitress who had been at his consecration luncheon asked the Cardinal as he left the banqueting room.

"Not half as good a one as you, Kitty," the Cardinal said, and meant it.

CHAPTER XXII

"*Eminentísimo Cardenal, somos siempre hermanos,*" His Most Illustrious Excellency Pedro Gonzalez y Casasrojas, *ci-devant* Padre Todo o Nada, said as he came waddling along the red carpeted station platform to embrace the Cardinal Archbishop of Inchkeith and the Pentlands, sent in 1956 as Papal Legate to the celebrations in honour of the septcentenary of San Firmín de las Estrellas.

" His Most Illustrious Excellency is telling the Most Eminent Cardinal that they are still brothers," the Archbishop's chaplain translated.

The Archbishop's face, the Cardinal saw, was now like a dried up lemon, but his brilliantined suffragans with their purple cloaks flapping in the wind like girls' dresses looked as young as sub-deacons. The Humpty Dumpty Canons however seemed as old as those who had been martyred: the Civil War, the Cardinal realised with a shock, had now been over for seventeen years.

" Tell me, Most Illustrious Excellency," he said. " Were there many priests killed in Your Most Illustrious Excellency's diocese during the trouble? "

" Two thousand three hundred and fifty-three, Most Eminent Lord Cardinal. And Princess Margaret? I hope that she is well."

" Thank you, Your Most Illustrious Excellency. To the best of my knowledge, I think so, yes."

" That is good news, my Lord Cardinal. It said in the *Diario de Madrid* that she had had to cancel her Inspection of First Battalion of the Fifeshire Light Infantry last week. And your most glorious writer the Illustrious Edgar Rice Burroughs? He has been writing more books about Tarzan, no? "

" We have another glorious writer now, Your Most Illustrious Excellency: the Illustrious Graham Greene."

" And, my Lord Cardinal, is the Illustrious Graham

Greene as good a writer as the Illustrious Edgar Rice Burroughs?"

"The *Sunday Times* and the *Observer* seem to think so, Your Most Illustrious Excellency, but the *Pentlands Evening Pibroch* is not so sure."

The Alcalde, festooned with ribbons like a horse at a fair, came forward to greet the Cardinal:

"The Generalísimo is a great friend of Scotland. The Generalísimo is also a great friend of God: in Spain 90% of those who die now receive the Last Sacraments."

"Not every one that saith unto me, Lord, Lord, shall enter into the kingdom of heaven; but he that doeth the will of my Father which is in heaven." None the less final unrepentance was still the sin against the Holy Ghost, and being brave enough to plump for God only when death was certain a sensible cowardice. Spain's 90% "Jesus, Murphy's" was better than France's 90% cocking snooks.

Bum-bum-bum, went the great big drum; toot-toot-toot, went the trumpets. The time was not for attempting to draw graphs of the incidence of grace; the time was for getting into the open Cadillac with His Most Illustrious Excellency.

"*Viva el Cardenal! Viva San Firmín! Viva la Santísima Padrona! Viva la Reina Isabel. Viva el Duque de Edimburgo. Viva la Princesa Margarita!*"

"And Pepita Gutierrez, Your Most Illustrious Excellency?" the Cardinal asked as he and Monsignor

Brodie drove off with the Archbishop and his chaplain. " Is she still receiving the stigmata every Friday afternoon ? "

" How should she not be, Most Eminent Lord Cardinal ? When God suspends a physical law He is just as consistent at breaking it as at keeping it. Tell me though, my Lord Cardinal: does Princess Margaret read the books of your new glorious writer Edgar Rice Greene ? "

Bum-bum-bum, went the great big drum; toot-toot-toot, went the trumpets.

" I am afraid that I am not in a position to answer that question, Your Most Illustrious Excellency. And His Late Most Illustrious Excellency, I hope that he did not suffer too much when he was killed by the Reds."

" On the contrary, Most Eminent Lord Cardinal, His Most Illustrious Excellency suffered a great deal. Before he was stripped naked and flung over the cliff he was strung up by the feet by chains and beaten with rubber truncheons. But he died bravely."

" And His Late Most Illustrious Excellency's cathedral chapter, Your Most Illustrious Excellency ? I have heard that they died bravely too."

"And how should they not, Most Eminent Lord Cardinal ? They knew that they were going to heaven, did they not ? "

Bum-bum-bum, went the great big drum; toot-toot-toot, went the trumpets. " *Viva el Cardenal!*

Viva la Princesa Margarita!" Scattering blessings at the cheering crowd, the Cardinal felt quite like Princess Margaret himself, although he didn't suppose that the Vicar-General would have described his elation as " authentic existence."

". . . BAJO EL IMPERIO DE LO ESPIRITUAL." Would either British Conservatives or Socialists have dared to put God before groceries on a banner in Bournemouth? How wrong Protestants were to imagine that in Spain Christ was stifled in Sacraments. How foolish were progressive Catholics: if a national Church could not make a whole population Christian it could at least make a whole population respect Christianity. Newman had gone even further: he had recommended, not that the Church should be a branch of the State, but that the State should be a branch of the Church.

Bum-bum-bum, went the great big drum; toot-toot-toot, went the trumpets. The Church wasn't only careless clergymen: Irish hobbledehoys, Spanish lazybones, Italian time-servers, French toe-the-liners. The Church was the immense hotch-potch of the baptised, longing to know or afraid to know. The Church was a thread of scarlet. The Church was a mirror held up. The Church was God's tent pitched on earth. Even at its grubbiest the Church was marked and the assertion made. Bum-bum-bum, went the great big drum; toot-toot-toot, went the trumpets.

"His present Most Illustrious Excellency is a too modest man," the Archbishop's chaplain said. "His present Most Illustrious Excellency was hanged like the English Martyrs at Tyburn and cut down before he was dead; but when the Reds saw how brave a man His Most Illustrious Excellency was they did not pull out His Most Illustrious Excellency's bowels and set fire to them."

Bum-bum-bum, went the great big drum; and toot-toot-toot, went the trumpets. "*Viva el Cardenal! Viva el Arzobispo! Viva el Alcalde! Viva la Princesa Margarita!*"

"And, Most Eminent Lord Cardinal," the Archbishop asked, "does the Illustrious Edgar Rice Greene also write about Tarzan?"

Bum-bum-bum, went the great big drum; toot-toot-toot, went the trumpets. Only seventeen of the band were out of step. Perhaps the Civil War had improved the discipline of Spanish priests too. Canons who had risked being thrown over cliffs for their faith couldn't but have learned a thing or two. Bum-bum-bum, went the great big drum; toot-toot-toot, went the trumpets.

2

"Doesn't the scab know it's Friday?" Monsignor Brodie asked, drawing the Cardinal's attention to a young Frenchman feeding roast chicken into the mouth of a fair haired girl in the hotel dining-room.

" You're allowed to eat meat on Friday in Spain," the Cardinal said. " There's a bull for it. Didn't you know ? "

" I'll bet you that fellow doesn't know either so he'll still go to hell."

" Anyway, Monsignor, there's no bull for blondes."

" Or for Archbishops wearing green *and gold* cords round their hats when the decree of 3rd November 1826 reserves the privilege to the four Latin Patriarchs. His Most Illustrious Excellency may be a brave man, Your Eminence, but he strikes me as being a bit of a dumb cluck."

" You mean, Monsignor, that His Most Illustrious Excellency is a bit of a dumb cluck but that he strikes you as being a brave man."

But the Cardinal didn't say this severely : he was still feeling too happy about the Church.

3

His Most Illustrious Excellency the Lord Archbishop of San Firmín de las Estrellas y Rio Largo didn't believe in using one word where a hundred would do, and in his sermon next day in the cathedral he was at the top of his form :

" Our most holy patron, the most holy San Firmín de las Estrellas, is the most holy of all the saints of holy Spain, holier much than San Firmín de Cast-

rogeriz, holier even than San Pedro de Villarejo de
Salvanés. It is because of this holiness of our most
holy patron that our Most Holy Father, the most
saintly Pius the Twelfth, has sent the Most Eminent
Donald Dunwhinnie Campbell, Cardinal of the Most
Holy Catholic, Apostolic and Roman Church,
Cardinal Priest and Protector of the Church of Saint
Babila-on-the-Appian Way, to represent him at the
most impressive celebrations which the most pious
people of San Firmín de las Estrellas y Rio Largo
are holding in honour of their most holy patron saint."

With their knave-of-diamonds birettas tipped down
over their faces to hide the thoughts about the
Universal Church they weren't having, the Humpty
Dumpty Canons of the chapter of the Most Holy
San Firmín de las Estrellas, whose miracles had been
such an eye-opener for San Firmín de Castrogeriz,
were already sound asleep in their stalls. The master
of ceremonies was flat out on the altar steps.

Had the baboons and the orang outangs learned
nothing after all, the Cardinal wondered. Had
watching other baboons and orang outangs being
spiked to death not taught the fools that if the Form
were to be allowed to survive it must be so choc-a-
block with Spirit that even its enemies would respect
it? Where were the young men, the Cardinal
wondered, looking over the nave crammed with
women jerking awake their weariness with fans. In
cellars, listening to short words full of meaning?

" And as from his glorious place in heaven, side by side with San Firmín de Castrogeriz, San Pedro de Villarejo de Salvanés and other most holy saints, confessors, martyrs, virgins and doctors of the Most Holy Catholic, Apostolic and Roman Church, our holy patron looks down upon this cathedral today, his heart must beat with love for the most pious people of San Firmín de las Estrellas y Rio Largo who have come out to do honour to their most holy patron."

The Cardinal rose with relief and intoned the first four words of the Creed.

4

The young men the Cardinal hadn't seen in the cathedral were all there for the eats in the Casas Consistoriales de la Muy Noble, Muy Leal y Muy Heroica Ciudad de San Firmín de las Estrellas. The Canons of the chapter of the most holy San Firmín were there too, wide awake now, pushing and shoving to get at the food before the laity. Outside, the band that had greeted the Cardinal was thumping and too-hooing away, and its rumpus came through to the notabilities whom the Alcalde was entertaining to sit-down luncheon in the room in which Isabel the Catholic had nearly slept a night.

" Did Your Eminence ever hear the story about His Illustrious Excellency the Bishop of Chinchilla de Monte-Aragón offering the Cardinal Archbishop of

Paris a *péché mortel* instead of a *pêche Melba* at the
Eucharistic Congress in Barcelona?" the Alcalde
asked the Cardinal.

"How much does a tram driver in the city earn?"
the Cardinal asked back.

"Fourteen pesetas a day, Your Eminence. Oh, no,
I remember now: we heard they were going to ask
for sixteen so we put it up to fifteen."

At the Hotel Maria Cristina the Cardinal and
Monsignor Murphy were paying two hundred
pesetas a day each.

"And rent?" the Cardinal asked on into the
surprised cold face. "What does he have to pay for
that?"

"Anything from fifty to seventy-five pesetas a
month, Your Eminence."

It wasn't as out of proportion as the Cardinal had
expected; but couldn't a shared lavatory on a stair
head obscure God almost as effectively as a Cardinal
and a Most Illustrious Excellency in a Cadillac?

"The Most Eminent Lord Cardinal must not make
the mistake of judging conditions in Spain by those
in his own country," the Archbishop said. "In Spain
there is always sunshine and oranges and our children
never suffer from rickets."

It was only in a climate like that of Palestine, the
Cardinal remembered Ernest Renan had said, that one
could obey the evangelical counsel of taking no
thought for the morrow. There were no locusts and

wild honey in Stockholm, and a chartered accountant would have a thin time of it trying to live like a lily of the field in the Archdiocese of Inchkeith and the Pentlands.

" And the Most Eminent Lord Cardinal must not forget that Spain has still to recover from her eight centuries' struggle against the Moor."

The Cardinal tried to forget his brother of Seville's tirades against dancing, Anglican chapels and *Wuthering Heights*. The Cardinal thought instead of the apostolic zeal of the Bishop of Malaga, of the high altar in the Escorial, of the new movement for Spanish laymen called *Opus Dei*. The Cardinal wanted to go on believing in the Church in Spain. The Cardinal wanted to be able to think that those who had their entrails torn out for God would stand a pinprick or two for their neighbour.

" Of course, Your Most Illustrious Excellency, we have our problems in Scotland too," and did his best to persuade himself that they were really as bad.

5

At night there were fireworks, and when the Cardinal and Monsignor Brodie took a walk along the sea front before going to bed the floodlit statue of the most holy patron on the hill towered over the bay like a monster *Wagons-Lits* ice. The Abbé Bonpapa was right, the Cardinal thought: electricity was more dangerous for religion than Bertrand Russell.

" Well, Monsignor," he asked. " What's the low down ? "

" The lift boy gets fifty pesetas a month and the run of his teeth; a lot of working people are living in sin because they can't afford the stole fees; and people who are too poor to pay the priest are buried like dogs."

In front of a poster for the bullfight by which the most holy patron was going to be honoured next day a ragged boy of seven was selling American cigarettes.

" My grandmother sends me out," he told the Cardinal when Monsignor Brodie had bought up his stock. " She says she can't keep me unless I help her."

Was this how the material conditions of a country were raised under the aegis of the spiritual, the Cardinal wondered as they walked back to their hotel under the spaced out tamarinds. How was it that men who were brave enough to die for Christ's teaching did not practise it ? Perhaps only Edgar Rice Greene could explain.

CHAPTER XXIII

SURPRISINGLY THE Vicar-General showed no jealousy when the Cardinal consecrated Monsignor Brodie Bishop of Olympus in the regions of the unfaithful: perhaps Monsignor Samson-Slingsby realised that at eighty-one he was too old to learn how to hold a crozier; or perhaps after all the only result of the 1955 mission in the cathedral had not been the maintenance with clergy's coffee of the demerara sugar which the Redemptorist had always asked for with his.

On the feast of St. Gregory Nazianzen 1956, in the pro-cathedral of St. Bean, the Cardinal and the Bishops of Glentulchan and Invergarbie gave Hector Roderick Douglas Gordon Brodie the Holy Ghost and the power to bestow it; and the Cardinal anointed his head and his hands, that he might be able to curse, to bless and to bind, to hate pride and to shun praise, and that the fragrance of his life might be as the dew of Hermon.

" Always remember what St. Paul wrote to Titus," the Cardinal told the new Bishop as he drove him to the official luncheon in the Ossian Hotel. " ' A bishop must be blameless, as the steward of God; not self-willed, not soon angry; not given to wine, no striker, not given to filthy lucre.' Don't imagine that just because you're a Bishop now you won't be able to preach the sort of twaddle that makes educated laymen lose their faith; all that the Holy Ghost can be counted on to do is to prevent our twaddle from degenerating into imbecility. Don't try to curry favour with the apathetic by aping their worldliness or with infidels by pretending to have read philosophers you haven't even heard of. Listen to Jesuits, Benedictines and Dominicans but take Franciscans and Oratorians with a pinch of salt. Pay proper attention to the liturgy, which is good manners towards God, but remember that sloppy hymns are to the illiterate what the photograph of his pudding faced wife is to the private soldier. Always publish audited accounts: the laity will always think you're cheating even when you aren't. Marry and bury poor people as well as rich people. Cocteau was only partially right: the last refuge of an original mind in an original age is not only conformity, but charity. And auxiliary Bishops do not repeat not play practical jokes on nuns."

CHAPTER XXIV

IN SPITE of his advice to Bishop Brodie the Cardinal himself was beginning to get careless about matters of liturgy: often he caught himself walking back to the centre of the altar before he had finished the " *per omnia saecula saeculorum* " at the end of a post-communion; once he let his thumb slip from his forefinger before the " *Qui pridie quam pateretur* "; and at the blessing of the oils on Holy Thursday he thrice sat down on the tail of his chasuble without waiting for the sub-deacon to hold it up.

He thought it as well therefore to accept the Abbé Bonpapa's suggestion that he should do a retreat at Solesmes.

Every morning for a week Dom Expédite stood in front of the Cardinal in a side chapel and pitched in.

The Cardinal, Dom Expédite told the Cardinal, had been sent into the world, not to be Archbishop of Inchkeith and the Pentlands and Cardinal Priest of Saint Babila-on-the-Appian Way, but to save his soul, which God had called into being from all eternity; to know God, to love God and to serve God. This was the only purpose of the Cardinal's existence as it was the only explanation of it. Heaven, hell, purgatory, these were the realities, and not the conjectures of Hegel and Kant. Did Spinoza stand a better chance than Christ of persuading a peasant to lighten his donkey's load? Could Bergson help a charwoman to die? The answer, as the Cardinal's great writer Evelyn Woog had pointed out, must be simple. It was and God had given it: baptism, penance, eucharist.

At the moment of death the opportunity for gaining merit would have passed as irrevocably for the Cardinal as for the beggar thrown to rot in the ditch; but because the Cardinal had dared to become a priesr and have the power put upon him a much severer accounting would be asked of him.

Had the Cardinal examined his conscience every night and asked forgiveness for his blunders, prides, omissions and cupidities? Had he always had mercy and been brave? How often had the Cardinal said the Lord's Prayer with a wish on every clause? How often had his thoughts wandered culpably during the celebration of Mass? Had the Cardinal's mission been less to convert unbelievers than to prevent unbelievers converting him? Had he connived at cruelty by not wishing to hear it spoken of, or imagined that injustice he didn't see was equity? Had the Cardinal's charity been for infidels and those not of his fold as well as for the faithful? Had he tried to tame Christ to his measure? Had he always had the goodwill to see the shimmer of the Church shining through other priests' faults and his own? Had love been insulated from his finger tips?

His Eminence however did not despair. Hope was the only one of the three theological virtues that one could brag about without spiritual pride. Hell might not, as St. Odo of Cluny had feared, be populated exclusively with clergymen. There might, Dom Expédite thought, be a few of the laity there too.

2

The Abbé Bonpapa, when the Cardinal met him in Paris, backed St. Odo's view, and quoted what the devil had said to the Abbé Donissan in *Sous le Soleil de Satan*.

"And Bernanos was right," the Abbé went on. "The devil kisses all us priests, whether we're lazy or on our toes all the time, dead or alive. We carry Lucifer in our entrails as surely as we carry Christ's Body when we leave the altar. Even poor old Armand Lucot stands a better chance than we do. He's dying in case you don't know. No priest of course. Apparently the Vicar Capitular himself went to see him but of course he was thrown out on his ear."

"And you, Monsieur l'Abbé?" the Cardinal asked. "Have *you* been to see him? After all you're his friend. You might be able to succeed where a stranger couldn't."

"I know my Gide better than that, Your Eminence.

' *La culture positive de Vincent le retenait de croire au surnaturel, ce qui donnait au démon de grands avantages.*' "

" You and your quotations," the Cardinal said. " Disbelief's apt to stop helping the devil on death-beds. Scotsmen know that if Frenchmen don't: every day of our lives we get bumpkins into heaven by the cartload. All the French clergy have been able to do is to spoon up Claudel."

" All right, Your Eminence," the Abbé Bonpapa said. " But don't say I didn't warn you."

3

The Cardinal was not thrown out on his ear like the Vicar Capitular, but to begin with the going was hard:

" I think I told Your Eminence forty years ago that I was unconvinced by the twenty-four shaky answers the Church gives to reason," the statesman whispered from his pillow. " I am still unconvinced by them. But I don't want Your Eminence to misunderstand me: I respect the Church of course, but . . ."

" Stop talking balderdash, will you? " the Cardinal shouted. " The only reason French politicians respect the Church is because the Church has helped them to colonise North Africa. Can't you forget you're a Radical Socialist for once? It won't matter what Reynaud and Daladier think when you're dead;

it'll only matter what God thinks. And what about the twenty-four shaky answers *you've* given *Him*? More like two hundred and forty, I expect, and most of them women, I'll bet."

The statesman did not answer, but a smile cracked the pain on his lips.

"You've lied and you've cheated all your life," the Cardinal went on. "And what's more I'm pretty certain you and your friends haven't read the writers whose fallacies you quote as a justification for having robbed your fellow countrymen of God. What you and your like have never understood is that religion hasn't only got to come down from heaven to earth; it's also got to go up from earth to heaven. ' But seek ye first the kingdom of God, and His righteousness, and all these things shall be added unto you.' If it hadn't been for Voltaire and Anatole France and their misinterpreters at forty removes you wouldn't have lost the war in 1940. However, Voltaire's and Anatole France's scepticism was at least honest and so they won't be sent to hell for it; but yours isn't and you will. And don't imagine that because there aren't any flames hell won't hurt. It'll hurt because when you arrive there you'll find out all of a sudden that you love God and you'll know that you've lost Him for ever and ever through your own fault. And hell's not only the absence either; it's also the presence: all your nasty political pals will be there too and all the two hundred and forty women . . ."

4

In gratitude for his having reconciled the statesman to the Church, this time the *Archevêché* authorised the Abbé Bonpapa to stand the Cardinal the whole shooting match at Chez Théophraste: hors d'œuvre, eggs, fish, dessert, meat and wine at eighteen hundred francs per nob.

"Well, Eminence, what do you know?" the Abbé Bonpapa said when they had chosen their meal. "What beats me is why the Archbishop of Paris didn't insist on rushing round himself in a taxi and converting him all over again. What with parish priests diving into tanks from tops of trees and Jesuits twanging guitars in the Vel' d'Hiver the hierarchy's not been doing so well lately. Of course the real answer to Françoise Sagan and Simone de Beauvoir is a Bishop who can drive a Jaguar faster than Stirling Moss or a Cardinal who can pee over the Eiffel Tower."

"Now, now," the Cardinal said. "You've got the Abbé Pierre, don't forget."

"It's thirty thousand Abbés Pierres we want if the rot's to be stopped. We'd have got them too with the Worker Priest Movement. But it was nipped in the bud by Rome. I know that heresies were spoken here and there, but the heresies could have been rooted out, couldn't they? ' *Surtout, mes enfants, pas d'histoires,*' the Bishops tell us now. ' Above all

234

let's have no unpleasantness.' Can you imagine St. Paul saying that to the Thessalonians? No wonder most young priests in France are beginning to lose heart."

" Surely things aren't as bad as all that, Monsieur l'Abbé," the Cardinal said gently.

" They're worse, Eminence, you don't understand. *Vous êtes Cardinal; vous n'êtes plus dans le bain.* And what's worse: the Pope's no longer in the bath either."

It went on like that, all through lunch.

5

Maynooth was not only still in the bath, but splashing over the side, the Cardinal thought that evening as his eye caught in the *Evening Standard* a list of books recently banned in the Irish Free State:

DOLLS ARE DYNAMITE by FREDERICK FOBEN
HER CANDLE BURNS HOT by HODGE EVANS
PRIVATE EYEFUL by NICK PERELLI
RED LIGHT BABE by DOUG DUPERAULT
TONIGHT, JOSEPHINE by LOLA LIMPROK
FREEWILL AND THE MOLECULE by the RIGHT
REVEREND MONSIGNOR ARTHUR SKIBO SAMSON-
SLINGSBY, V.G.

The Cardinal was on the next train to Rome.

CHAPTER XXV

" WHAT BRINGS you here this time, Eminentissimo?"
Cardinal Pantachini asked. "Another miracle in
Your Eminence's Archdiocese? Or more grumbles
about San Firmín de las Estrellas? I'd give up if I were
you: to make Spanish priests observe rubrics tanks
and a secret police are required."

But the Cardinal knew that behind the leathery
impenetrability of his expression Miss Assisi had
guessed that His Eminence of Inchkeith and the
Pentlands had got wind of the trouble that was brew-
ing for him.

" I have come to see His Holiness about a private
matter," he said.

" Your Eminence is indeed fortunate. Most of us
find it difficult to see His Holiness about *public* matters
these days."

The Cardinal knew that Miss Assisi spoke the truth:
even Bishops were no longer sure of a private audience,
and a lifetime of devotion might be rewarded only
by a passing smile from the Boss.

" That's just the point, Eminentissimo," he said.
" I haven't got an appointment, and I was wondering
if Your Eminence . . ."

" As a member of the Curia, Eminentissimo, it is not my business to arrange for audiences. That, as Your Eminence must know, is done through the Secretariat."

" I do know, Eminentissimo; but I thought that perhaps with Your Eminence's influence . . ."

" His Holiness, Eminentissimo, is very fully booked for at least a month. Today he has the Abbot General of the Benedictines, the Brazilian Ambassador, the Prima Ballerina of the Scala, the Mother General of the Helpers of the Holy Souls . . ."

The Cardinal gently slid a white carton across the desk.

". . . Lucky Strike, Eminentissimo ? My favourites. However did Your Eminence guess ? "

" A little bird told me, Eminentissimo," the Cardinal said.

2

The Cardinal was received by the Pope immediately after the winner of the Milan-San Remo cycle race.

" From where you come, Eminence ? " the Pope asked after he had blessed the Cardinal and embraced him. " Tell me about."

The Cardinal did not beat about the bush.

" Holiness," he said. " This book of my Vicar-General's. It's a serious work. It's not as though it were *Forever Amber*."

" Is that another book of the Monsignor Samson-Slingsby, Eminence? If so I shall ought to ask the Holy Office to read."

No wonder Wiseman had never been able to explain the Church of England to Pius IX, the Cardinal thought.

" It was just an instance I was taking, Holiness," he said. " I was trying to show that there is no similarity at all between my Vicar-General's book and the type of novel the Irish Free State Censors have bracketed it with."

" Your Eminence need have no fears on that score as far as the Holy Office is concerned." The Pope was speaking Italian now, and not at all benevolently. " In Our view it is heresy that is the dynamite and for that reason Monsignor Samson-Slingsby's book will not be bracketed with any others when We condemn it." Opening a drawer in his desk, the Pope took out a copy of *Freewill and the Molecule* and clapped it down in front of the Cardinal open at the title page. " Fourteen major heresies, Our Assessor, Comissary and Vice-Commissary tell us," he said and pointed at:

IMPRIMATUR.

DONALDUS DUNWHINNIE CARDINALIS CAMPBELL
ARCIEPISCOPUS INCHKEITHIENSIS
DIE 24A JUNII 1955

The Cardinal was too unhappy even to think of

drawing the Pope's attention to what was printed at the bottom of the page opposite:

CHUBB, SKATE and APPLETREES,
Publishers to the Holy See
LONDON, MELBOURNE TORONTO

" No *Censor Deputatus* either," the Pope said.

" I know, Your Holiness; but you see none of my clergy are educated enough to understand Monsignor Samson-Slingsby's sometimes rather involved thought."

" And Your Eminence is? All right, tell me: ought the notional *moi* of Sartre to be added to, or subtracted from, the cogitational *ego* of Descartes ? "

Was that the bit *l'en soi* and *le pour soi* had come into, or wasn't it? An Archbishop was supposed to know so many things these days, and already the Cardinal had forgotten what he had said about them when he had been showing off at the Artists' Institute dinner. He would just have to chance his arm and hope that the Pope didn't know either.

" Added," he said.

" Neither added nor subtracted," the Pope said. " Both are erroneous conceptions of identity." But the big black eyes floating behind the thick wheels of spectacle were smiling. " ' The imbecility of profound philosophers is so immense that it is surpassed only by God's mercy.' Papini, Your Eminence. ' Only God, because He is God, has the right to be an atheist,' he also wrote. What a pity I had to put a man like that on the Index."

The Cardinal sat humbly in silence.

" Believe me, Your Eminence, we are as concerned about the partial righteousness of Our children as are Your Eminence and Your Eminence's Vicar-General. But We shall never improve things unless We strike the evil at its root: heresy, from which stems the religious illiteracy so common in the English-speaking world today. Even in their free-masonry of hating Christ, God's enemies do not seem to be able to love one another. And they never will love one another, Eminence, until they have had the courage to free themselves from the tyranny of liberty."

How wrong Peyrefitte had been, the Cardinal thought: if this wasn't the Holy Ghost speaking, it certainly wasn't Suora Pasqualina.

" Heresy, Your Eminence, breeds first the will to disbelieve and then the will to disobey. Your Eminence may say that Voltaire has taught the world that already, but it is important that people should not be more hardly cemented in their errors by hearing the wrong things from the right people. That is why We have had to call the French Worker Priest Move-ment to order, and that is why We shall place Your Eminence's Vicar-General's book on the Index."

" I understand, Holiness," the Cardinal said. " But if Your Holiness could see your way to letting him down lightly. To my own certain knowledge Monsignor Samson-Slingsby has worked for nearly fifty years on that book."

" We shall exercise clemency; Your Eminence may rest assured of that. Whatever their failings or their excellences, We love all our children in the world equally, without favour or predilection. ' Judge not, that ye be not judged,' Your Eminence. We should remember that we are all of us prone to condemn others for exactly those turpitudes we are blind to in ourselves."

Was this a dig about what he had said to Miss Assisi about Spain? Or was the Pope seeing right down inside his Cardinal? Was His Holiness trying to tell His Loyal Son of Inchkeith and the Pentlands that St. Peter Damian would never have tried to bribe his way into Stephen IX by slipping a leg of mutton to a member of his Curia?

" Things are perhaps better than Your Eminence thinks, even here in Italy. In the hospitals founded by Giuseppe Benedetto Cottolengo more than twelve thousand epileptics, hydrocephalics, dwarfs, orphans and paupers are looked after by priests and nuns who spend daily on them all the money they receive and never lack for more. In his summer residence the Cardinal Archbishop of Bologna sits down to table with the poor working boys he shelters in his palace. In Milan cancerous growths are cured instantaneously by intercession at Cardinal Schuster's tomb. All over the world, Eminence, in high places and in low, God has His secret saints; and as we can never read what goes on in the hearts of those we meet, it is our duty to treat them as holier than ourselves, whose faults we know. Although for Our own part We are disinclined to imagine that either Your Eminence's Sir Winston Churchill or King George the Fifth was thinking exclusively about his salvation when they met at Cowes in 1887, it is Our obligation in charity, and not just as heaven's diplomat, to comport Our thoughts towards them as though We know that they were. Kierkegaard, whom Your Eminence's Vicar-General quotes so often, says that a genius should be ' nailed out in isolation.' That is how it should be with a Pope, Your Eminence, and with a Cardinal Archbishop too. *Benedictio Dei Omnipotentis, Patris, et Filii, et Spiritus Sancti, descendat super te et maneat semper.* And I don't only give you my blessing, Your Eminence. I give you my love as well, and I mean it."

CHAPTER XXVI

NOWADAYS BISHOP BRODIE as well as the Vicar-General helped the Cardinal with his Christmas cards: the Auxiliary checked the 1956 outgoing list against the 1955 incoming list; Monsignor Samson-Slingsby, very humble since the condemnation of *Freewill and the Molecule*, wrote the addresses on the envelopes; and the Cardinal refereed.

" Miss Assisi get a card this year, Your Eminence ? " Bishop Brodie asked. " The one he sent last year had the Cardinal Archbishop of Naples's signature showing through under his."

" Send him one all the same," the Cardinal said.

" And Father Eutychus Gilhooley, Your Eminence ? Who's he when he's at home ? "

" A brown job," the Vicar-General said. " And what's more he's not at home. He's on this new Franciscan stunt of driving steamrollers from Paris to Bilbao in order to keep in with the great heart of the people."

" The card Sister Scholastica sent last year had ' Esso ' on it, Your Eminence."

" Send them all cards," the Cardinal said and turned back to his newspaper:

" I send my blessing to the Hungarian weapons that have won this glorious victory. God will bless those weapons which have brought us our freedom in our dire day of need."

If God would bless the weapons why did Cardinal Mindzenty need to ? If God wouldn't how did Cardinal Mindzenty dare to ? Could disillusioned Communists' tommy guns be the voice of the gospel any more than Franco's cannons ?

" Old Sambo Wumerumbani, Your Eminence? That's two years running now he hasn't sent a card. Too busy with kerygmatic catechesis probably."

" Drop him, Hector," the Cardinal said. " After all we haven't *three* cheeks to turn."

And yet, the Cardinal wondered, would he himself, if he had been shut up for six years in the bottle dungeon at St. Andrews, have been able to refrain from tracing a sign of the Cross over the skean-dhus of Argyll and Sutherland Highlanders who set him free to say Mass again?

What a good thing it was that there was the mathematic of faith to protect the Church against the off-the-cuff pronouncements of her Cardinal Archbishops.

2

Although he was now seventy-three the Cardinal still went down to the cathedral on Christmas Eve to help out with confessions.

" Keeping the lassie's telephone number is scarcely indicative of a firm purpose of amendment," Father O'Leary was bawling in the box next door as the Cardinal slid back the grille and blessed a pink hat.

" Please, Your Eminence, I havena sinned."

The Anglican liturgy had hit at least one nail on the head, the Cardinal thought as he paraphrased the Book of Common Prayer:

" Even if you have not done those things which you ought not to have done, my child, you must have left undone some of those things which you ought to have done. How long is it since your last confession ? "

" Five minutes, Your Eminence. I just wanted to wish Your Eminence a Happy Christmas, that's all."

And the pink hat was gone before he could wish it one back.

3

The Cardinal presided from the throne at the Pontifical High Mass of Midnight, sung from the faldstool by His Lordship the Bishop of Olympus, and assisted from the tribune at the Pontifical High Mass of the Aurora sung by Monsignor Samson-Slingsby, who had now been made a pronotary apostolic and was allowed to wear a mitre.

The Cardinal himself sang the Pontifical High Mass of Noon, and preached the sermon, taking his text from the gospel for the Fourth Sunday after the Epiphany: " *Quid timidi estis, modicae fidei*." " Why are ye fearful, o ye of little faith ? "

The Church, the Cardinal said, was like the ship which Jesus had entered into with His disciples. Once again the great tempest had arisen in the sea and the Church was covered with waves as the ship had been. Even although it might often look as though Our

Lord were asleep again they must not lose heart. As before the winds and the sea would obey Him, but in His own good time. In the meanwhile they must not be afraid as the disciples had been, because their delivery now could not be far off: already the signs were beginning to be seen in the sun and in the moon and in the stars, with the distress of nations now upon the earth, and men withering away for fear.

When the Mass was over the Cardinal unvested at the throne and left the cathedral by the west door. A few of the faithful had remained and a gang of roughnecks came out from the ice-cream parlour to gawk. The Cardinal was so busy blessing them that he scarcely had time to notice that he was still walking hentoed.

4

" Would you believe it, Your Eminence," Bishop Brodie said as they sat down to lunch. " Old Sambo Wumerumbani has sent a card after all. It came by the midday post."

" A telegram back, I think," the Cardinal said. " *Propaganda Fide* petty cash. After all His Eminence has promoted *my* faith: I can now believe I've got three cheeks."

But it was to the pink hat that the Cardinal really wanted to send a telegram.

CHAPTER XXVII

The Neapolitan club-sandwich of soap on the washstand was the first thing the Cardinal saw when he entered the Vicar-General's bedroom to give him Extreme Unction.

"They're apostolic stickers really," the Vicar-General said. "I pinched the first from Vaughan the day he ordained me. I don't suppose I've been a very good Christian since, but I don't think I've ever quite said 'no.'"

"I'm sure, Monsignor, I'm sure," the Cardinal said.

"And I ask Your Eminence's pardon for all the spite and jealousy I've always had against you, and from the very day I first set eyes on you too."

"Now, now, Monsignor, I don't suppose I've always been perfect either."

"Anyway, Your Eminence, I've left you my Clos Vougeot to make up."

Was this the turbulent priest of whom he had so often wished to be rid? Was this the cold cleric who used to preach to children that the first communion they were going to make was the greatest event of their lives, and then hare back to the presbytery for breakfast without waiting to see them make it?

As the Cardinal anointed the dying man he felt that Dom Expédite would have approved of his finger-tips.

CHAPTER XXVIII

WHEN CARDINAL PANTACHINI consecrated the new sanctuary of St. Bean's cathedral on Sunday within the Octave of the Ascension 1957 he made only four major mistakes in ritual. Preaching in English, Miss Assisi told the faithful how glad the Pope would be to learn how suggestive a cathedral His Eminence the Cardinal Archbishop of Inchkeith and the Pentlands had now acquired for himself. His Holiness would like people all over the world to save up and buy their Archbishops suggestive cathedrals.

To keep off his own face the grin which he saw on Bishop Brodie's, the Cardinal thought of what the Old Jock had said in Westminster Cathedral fifty years ago: "The straight line, the gentle fold, the clear prayer, that's what makes for devotion." It was only when the cooks from Rome came along to spoil the broth that noise, and not love, resounded in God's ear.

2

" Mixed choirs, Eminentissimo," Miss Assisi said that evening. " I take it that your parish priests have been instructed to place the women singers in separate galleries from the men."

" This is not the panting heart of Rome, Eminentissimo," the Cardinal answered. " Besides my women singers are so ugly they'd be safe even in St. Peter's."

" Your Eminence is pleased to jest. Now what about this night club . . . ? "

" The Moulin Tartan was closed a year ago, Eminentissimo, when the Town Council learned that the dance hostesses were flinging their breakfasts at one another's heads."

" And this Thistle Hotel where one goes for a lark, Eminentissimo? Has it been closed too? "

" Of course not. Why should it be? "

" In that case, Eminentissimo, I think that I should like to see this hotel where one goes for a lark. Perhaps Your Eminence and I could dine there tonight."

After all, the Cardinal asked himself, why not? The *Propaganda Fide* petty cash could stand it as well as the wire to Cardinal Sambo, and the charge would be even more appropriate, propagating the Pope's faith in His loyal son the Archbishop of Inchkeith and the Pentlands's propagation of it.

" Black suits, of course, Eminentissimo," he said.

" We don't want to rock the Church of God too much."

But the only sign of worldliness in the Sinners' Lounge was a spectacled young woman reading the *Scottish Episcopalian Monitor.*

" The lark, Eminentissimo," Cardinal Campbell said as he led his guest to a table.

" A Johnny Haig for me, Eminentissimo," Cardinal Pantachini said as a waitress came up.

" I'm sorry, but on the sabbath we're only allowed to serve drinks to residents of the hotel and bony feedy travellers," the waitress said.

" My friend's come from Rome, miss, and he's going back," the Cardinal said.

" In that case I'd like to have a see of his return ticket."

" *L'ho lasciato in casa.*"

" My friend says he's left his ticket at home, miss."

" Fine ham ! "

" But, miss . . ."

" Trying it on like that ! And both of you ministers too ! " the waitress said and stalked away.

" Don't worry, Eminentissimo," the Cardinal said. " We'll be served in the dining-room all right."

The Jezebel Grill was closed but the Gay Paree Brasserie was filled with red faced men and women whose bodies looked as though they were tweed all the way through."

" Are you two still being good Kartholics now ? "

250

the Cardinal's old friend the flat-footed waitress asked as she handed them menu cards.

" His Eminence is doing his best, I'm sure, Kitty," the Cardinal said, " and I'm doing my best to do my best."

" What will Your Eminences be having now ? The roast chicken's off, the roast lamb's off, the beef olives are off, but the mince collops and the sausage and mash are still on."

" A sausage and smash for me, Eminentissimo, I think," Cardinal Pantachini said.

" And you'll be keeping His Other Eminence company, Your Eminence, won't you ? "

" Yes, Kitty. And two double Haig and Haigs."

" Two sausages and mash and two double Haig and Haigs for their Lordships the Eminent Cardinals," Kitty shouted down the hatch.

A few crimson faces switched round to stare and then turned back again to their plates and their conversations:

" All you've got to do is to let go of both wrists at the same time."

" And then on the seventeenth green what did he do but lay me a stymie ! "

" Both thumbs down the club and make sure of your follow-through, McNab says."

" Give me the Strip-Tease and Casanova in Rome any day of the week, Eminentissimo," Cardinal

251

Pantachini said. " *There's* something worth writing an Encyclical about."

" I'm sorry to have disappointed you, Eminentissimo," Cardinal Campbell said. " We haven't any posters of Brigitte Bardot or Anita Ekberg either, I'm afraid, but I think I can rustle up a few Jesuits smoking."

" Now, now, Eminentissimo, remember what happened last time," Miss Assisi said.

But they were both of them smiling: they were old men now, and learning how to put up with each other's foibles.

CHAPTER XXIX

ON THE Feast of Saints Peter and Paul 1957 the Cardinal passed on the certainty to six raw young deacons and ordained them priests; knowing that it wouldn't be long before the reminder in the sacristy for the *Te igitur* read:

NOMEN ARCIEPISCOPI:

HECTOR,

he tried to speak to them as he thought the Old Jock would have done.

The Form, he told them, must contain the Spirit and the Spirit fill the Form. If the religion *about*

Jesus required to be watered by the religion *of* Jesus, charity often withered without doctrine. Although their heroisms need not always outweigh their prudences, they must know when to choose the hot-water bottle and when the thumbscrew. They must not allow their celibacy to chill their souls. They must rid the world of the spectacle of kindness coming more often from unbelievers than from priests. The answer was not a George Bernard Shaw at West-minster or an Aneurin Bevan in the Vatican; the answer was their own subordination and the calm which it would give to those who beheld it.

CHAPTER XXX

IN DECEMBER 1957 the Cardinal no longer had to choose between a shave and a meditation: now that he had an electric razor the Cardinal could do both at once.

Was it, he could wonder even while stretching his chin, was it because of a desire to postpone the accounting that he was obeying the doctor and taking things easy?

Was it not at his own hesitations that his high falutin' pastorals had been aimed? What could a byre-boy in Cupar-Angus know of Jacques Maritain?

Had he looked long enough into stupid faces to

love the unhappiness behind them? Had he found loving his enemies easier than loving his friends only because he had had to see his friends as well?

Had he been glad when that grandstand had collapsed at that bullfight in Spain and the spectators been gored? Had his condemnation of the cruelty to animals not been a hypocrisy when his own enjoyment of bacon had never been spoiled by his delegated murder of the pig?

Had he been sorry that that dramatic critic hadn't been in the Catalina crash only because his death would have meant one sneer less? Hadn't he wished, not only that the critic might have been killed, but that he might have been killed in a state of mortal sin, and the hell he was sent to torture, absence and presence: flames, loss of God and listening to the literary boys talking about Kafka and Brecht all rolled into one?

Had he been grateful enough to God for decent Protestants who still went to church?

Had he condemned Angry Young Men and been an Angry Old Man himself?

Had he followed Chesterton's prescription for a priest and touched with a blessing those whom others wouldn't touch with a barge pole?

Had he hated in the Lord as well as loved in the Lord?

How often had he dared to walk out to God's grace without an umbrella up?

Had he, even when he was old, been, like the Old Jock, a lantern through which Christ shone out?

How was he going to answer the question from the liturgy of St. John Chrysostom: "Have I taken care to seek a blameless life and a good defence before the dread judgment seat of Christ?"

It was while the Cardinal was examining his conscience like this that he had his stroke, and after that High Mass at St. Bean's was no longer a colonel's parade.

2

When Bishop Brodie administered the Last Sacraments on *Gaudete* Sunday the Cardinal was too weak to scour his soul any more. All he could do was to lie still and think. He thought of those whom he had loved with all his heart: the Old Jock, the Cardinal Bishop of Minnehaha, Sister Scholastica, the Abbé Bonpapa, Miss Assisi, Pope Pius XI, Pope Pius XII, Kitty with the flat feet, His Most Illustrious Excellency Todo o Nada, Bishop Brodie, who would so soon rule Inchkeith and the Pentlands; and of the Church too, he thought, while there was still time: the Church was as God had always known it could only be, crouched down among hate, pride, cruelty and lust, and if ten per cent of the baptised listened to her teaching it was bogey.

"Into thy hands, O Lord, I commend my spirit,"

the Cardinal murmured. Mercy would probably be shown to those who hadn't relied on it too much, and perhaps a " Jesus, Murphy " sneaked one in after all. He had a right, Dom Expédite had said, to pat himself on the back for hoping.